THE HISTORY OF
POLLY BOWLER

THE HISTORY OF POLLY BOWLER

by Herself

As told to Keith Dewhurst

GREENHEART PRESS

First published in Great Britain 2021
by Greenheart Press

Copyright © Keith Dewhurst 2021

Keith Dewhurst has asserted his moral right to be identified as author of this Work in accordance with sections 77 and 78 of the Copyright, Designs and Patents Act 1988

All rights reserved. No part of this work may be reproduced, stored in a retrieval system, or transmitted, in any form or by any means, electronic, mechanical, photocopying, recording otherwise, without the prior written permission of the publisher.

A CIP catalogue record for this book is available from the British Library

ISBN 978-0-9571829-3-6

Produced by The Choir Press
Cover design by Paul Baker, A Stones Throw Design

For Alexandra

and in memory of Johnno

Keith Dewhurst in Publication

PLAYS
Rafferty's Chant in 'Plays of the Year'
Lark Rise to Candleford
War Plays (Corunna!, The World Turned Upside Down, The Bomb in Brewery Street)
Don Quixote
Black Snow
Philoctetes (translation)

TELEVISION
Running Milligan in 'Z-Cars'
Last Bus in 'Scene'

NOVELS
Captain of the Sands
McSullivan's Beach

THEATRE MEMOIR
Impossible Plays (with Jack Shepherd)

FOOTBALL
When You Put on a Red Shirt: Memories of Matt Busby, Jimmy Murphy and Manchester United
Underdogs: The Unlikely Story of Football's First F.A. Cup Heroes

KEITH DEWHURST was born in 1931 and worked in a cotton mill and as a journalist before becoming a playwright. Three of his seventeen stage plays were premiered at the Royal Court Theatre and six at the National Theatre. He wrote two movies, eighteen TV plays and episodes for many series, including the original 'Z-Cars'.

CHAPTER ONE

We were happiest when it was the four of us, Father and Mother and Jem and me. There must have been cold rainy days, because the village was half-way up the moor, but I don't remember any. What I remember are hazy summer evenings when noises were muffled but still carried a long way and Mother said "The men are coming round to practice football."

They ran and sweated, and laughed when they bumped into each other, and Father had his sly grin and told us that he was the best player, although I don't suppose now that he was. But they ran through the dusk and into the moonlight, and we were sent to bed but could still hear them, and hear Mother call "William, William. Come in, lad", and they stopped and she gave them bread and cheese, and beer that she had brewed herself, just as she'd baked the bread, and the milk came from our own cow.

Down the valley the new spinning machines we called throstles, because the spindles whistled as they turned, made more and more twist for the handlooms. We had two, one in the house and one in the stall where the horse had been, and it did not matter that our fields were neglected. There was so much work for the looms that what we did not grow or make for ourselves we were able to buy.

It was a good time, even if I did see it through childish eyes, but when I was eight or nine, and Jem six, it was over. It wasn't only throstles that could be driven by water, but power-looms, and men like Mr Shorrock built more mills along the river.

When Father was a lad he had stood in the river and caught salmon, but the scummy waste from paper and dye works had put paid to that, and now no-one sent twist to be woven on hand-looms because they were slower than the mills, and more expensive.

Men still came sometimes to play football, but more often to raise angry voices. Some wanted to break into the mills and smash the power looms, and one night they did. Jem and me weren't supposed to know, but we guessed and pretended we hadn't. We tried to stay awake, but drifted and woke up early, when Father and Mother were agitated and Mother said "Ssh!" to him, and he was impatient and said "But we showed 'em! We showed 'em alright!"

That's how he was, deft at the loom but clumsy sometimes, rushing at things like Jem, except that Jem thinks about it first without saying. When I remember Father in the light of the life we have lived, I think that he was huge-hearted, but not as clever as he thought he was.

Mother had made gruel for breakfast but before we finished it we heard shouting outside and it was Walter O'Jacks, out of breath and sweaty, come bow-legged from the village to say that soldiers had been sent for.

"Well, they can't shoot us in our own country," said Father, but they would have done, I think, if people had resisted.

As it was, those who had been warned ran away, so that by the time the soldiers came up to our yard Father had gone. The officer had a cold and kept blowing his nose and said "Don't come near me, Mrs Hindle, I don't want to pass it on." Then he demanded an item of Father's clothing so that the dogs could sniff and follow his scent. But Mother was cunning.

Father's brother Uncle Harry had been over from Manchester and left a shirt behind, and Mother gave that to the dogs. They buried their snouts in it and then set off, to follow the path Uncle Harry had taken. When they lost it, we heard later, the officer assumed that Father had escaped across the moors, and so did we, because he did not return and there was no news.

Mother had been defiant when the soldiers left, chin up, her voice sharp when she commanded our dog Trafalgar to stay and not romp after the others, and she was wonderful with Jem that night. She refused to let him sleep in her bed but went and lay in his, just for this one special time, mind. Then she warned us that Father had been a ring-leader, and that if they caught him they would put him on trial and as likely as not send him to Australia.

Jem said that he'd like to see Australia (he still would) but Mother said "Gingerbread Land's much better." There might be silence for months, she said, but if we were lucky Father would hide, and send for us later, to live another life somewhere else. This settled Jem and he closed his eyes. Mother mouthed me a kiss and blew out the taper.

In the dark I realised that what I did know for certain was that eighteen months earlier she had miscarried, a gush of blood and slime as she planted potatoes, and that now she was on her own, without Father, and five months into another pregnancy. I felt afraid, and the next morning was worse.

It was as though Mother had not slept at all, but lain wide awake like me, and repeated in her mind every problem that faced us, and been crushed. She was listless but scolding, and I thought: I've lost her. I don't know what to do without her. I did not want her to see my tears and went outside. She did not follow me but Trafalgar did, and I knelt in the dirt and hugged him and smelled his doggy smell, and he licked my face.

I said "If you love me we'll be safe because we've got to do it, Trafalgar, it's up to you and me." I thought that if we could endure the next week Mother would find herself again.

She could work a loom, and there were still some bits of work, but I reckoned that they might not suffice. I had always helped on the looms, crawling underneath to attach the warp to the beams, and I helped with the planting, digging and the animals. But I had never travelled further than the village, or the top of the moors where we watched hawks and dabbled in boggy little pools. I'd never seen more people together than those who sang in the chapel, and never studied more than the letters and numbers the Preacher's wife taught us at Sunday school, although we did own books: one of nursery rhymes, and a Bible, and a book about voyages and Africa, but the voyages weren't real to me, and neither was Africa. They may as well have been invented, and I had been so happy that I never thought about the future.

I knew now that I must. I must earn money. I must go all day to the mill, five in the morning until nine at night, and work for money.

"Polly, it won't be enough," said Mother.

"Jem can come with me. Bobbin boy."

"You don't understand," she said. "It isn't just what we need every week. It's that your Father owed money."

"Can't we send to Uncle Harry?"

Her smile was twisted.

"It's him that's owed the money," she said. "Now do you see?"

But we did manage to get along. Jem and me went to work in the mill, and Trafalgar kept our spirits up. Then winter came, and with it the day on which the worst happened.

CHAPTER TWO

"Be sharp," said Mother. "Look at that hour glass. Be sharp."
Jem struggled into his shirt and I thought: she's too tired to help him. She can't help him. So I helped him myself, but I watched her, and even in the rush-light she was waxy pale, and her stomach stuck out lower than yesterday, I thought.

"Come on Jem," I said, "Come you on," but he wanted to play with Trafalgar.

It was cold and not proper light outside, and the loom at the end of the room looked like a gallows.

"I've lost my comb," I said.

Jem had stuck it in his own hair. He put out his tongue and made a daft farting noise.

Did I want to giggle or hit him? I did neither, because Mother was slumped on the loom bench and said "Jem Hindle, don't behave like an half-baked boggart."

He started to say that even field-mice knew that boggarts looked like white horses.

Mother heaved for breath but made herself speak up.

"Take his dinner in your cloth," she said.

"Already have," I replied.

Already. Cheese and an onion. The last of the cheese, because three weeks before we'd sold the cow.

I hate to feel untidy and I combed my hair. Then I grabbed an old shawl and was wilful: I saw that Mother was too lost in herself to argue about clogs and I ran to the door without them. The way down from the fold was muddy slush, and I'd be numbed, but I hated clogs. I've always wanted to feel dainty, and to come and go gracefully, without clatter.

"Look to him, Polly," Mother called, as she always did, and "I will" I shouted back as I always did, because Jem was honest and loving but small, a rush-at-it lad who needed an eye kept on him.

As we went down the track snow blew in the wind, single flakes that stung and melted. Not much of the dawn had come over the moors yet, but there were lights in the windows of the mill below, and when we came to the first cottages people stumbled half-awake around us. Their clogs rattled on the cobbles that had been laid around the mill to give the wagons purchase, and I smelled the coal fire in the watch-house. I don't think that men and boys smell as keenly as we women, do you?

"Horse," said Jem, as Mr Shorrock swung down and handed over the reins. Mr Shorrock had a scarf around his shoulders and another under his chin and over the top of his hat. He always had a glint in his eye.

"Morning, Polly," he said, as he untied his scarves.

"Morning, Mr Shorrock," I said.

Father had hated Mr Shorrock, and said that he was cruel, but to me he always seemed sad, as though he had what he wanted, but needed something else that he would never find.

"Have you seen your Father?" he said.

"How d'you mean?" I said.

"It's blown over," said Mr Shorrock. "Tell your Mother I said that she should tell him not to be so daft, and come home."

What did he mean? Did he think that Mother met Father at night and in secret? Did he know that they had done so? If they had, would Jem and me not have known?

Jem was wary of Mr Shorrock. He tugged my sleeve and said "We'll be late." Mr Shorrock had a wry smile and said

"So will I, by heck," and we ducked away and up the outside steps to the top room.

"You're late," said the Number One Overlooker, who we all called Grumpyguts.

"No, I'm not."

"You're all but."

"I was delayed by Mr Shorrock," I said.

"Always got an answer, you have," said Grumpyguts.

My feet were cold and I said "Give us a rub, Jem," which he did saying "What did he mean, Polly? What did Mr Shorrock mean?"

"Don't let Grumpyguts hear you."

"But what did—?"

"Ssh ...! He's kind. That's all. I think he's a kind man."

Then bang went the sluice gate on the little river below us, and we heard water rush and the wheel begin to turn, and the rattle and slap of wheels and driving belts, and Grumpyguts blew a whistle, which meant that the throstles were ready to go.

Our spinner was old Ezekiel Chadwick, and much of the time he sat in a chair against the wall, and watched us children and Mrs Clough piece up on his machines. Shorrock paid Chadwick and Chadwick paid us, piece-work rates that we scurried for, and that morning me and Jem belted on our machines at once, because we'd been sensible and stayed back the previous night to bobbin up and be ready.

"Think you're bloody clever, you two!" yelled Grumpyguts, and by way of spite he snuffed out the wicks before it was properly light, so that it was harder for us to see when we pieced up broken threads. We stopped one machine altogether, which annoyed old Ezekiel, but he shouted back at Grumpyguts and came to help us, so it was quicker in the long run.

We kept our heads down and hoped that Grumpguts

wouldn't cuff us behind Ezekiel's back, but really we were used to it because it was an argument they had every day and once I remember Mr Shorrock himself came up and told them to stop behaving like tin pot Napoleons.

Anyway, it was about an hour after that day's saving-money-on-lamp-oil argument when young Willie Ashton the mill cashier came up. He pointed at me, brushed floating lint off his black waistcoat, and talked to Grumpyguts above the racket of the machines. Grumpyguts gestured: come here!

"What's up?" mouthed Ezekiel, and young Willie shouted in his ear.

Grumpyguts knocked the belts off our machines, grabbed my arm, and shoved me through the door.

Trafalgar was in the yard. He barked and howled and pawed at people, ran away and back again, and barked again. Then he saw me and bounded up the steps. He knocked me so that I sat down, and wrapped my arms around his head. He whimpered and I felt his heart pound. Then he barked and wriggled free. He jumped down to where Mr Shorrock had arrived and said "If I know anything about dogs he's come with a message," and gestured to me to follow Trafalgar, in my bare feet, through the slush, up the hill and into our yard, where Mother lay like rags, dead in the blood around the half-born baby that was dead as well, throttled by his own cord, and I looked round for Jem but he wasn't there.

They must have held him back at the mill and I was glad of it. He mustn't see her like this, I thought. By this time other people had run up and he never did see her in that state, but only as a stranger in the coffin. How fine she must have been when she was young, I thought, as we put a spray of last year's dead leaves on her bosom, because that was all we had.

It was a childish thought, because the fact is that she was young when she died, almost as young as I am now, when people have written that I am the most beautiful actress in Europe. I am her spitting image, Jem says, and reader, if what interests you is my fame, bear with me. But for that day when Trafalgar came with a message I would never have set foot upon a stage. I would never have left the mill, or the moorland valley village that became a town. When it was the four of us, Father and Mother and Jem and me, we were happy, and no applause, I have discovered, can bring that back.

CHAPTER THREE

Much of what children discover is overheard, is it not, spoken across them, or muttered, or conveyed by facial expressions and long words that grown-ups think no-one else understands. People like the Preacher's wife were kind to me and Jem, but in a meaningful sort of way, as though there was something that we were too young to understand; or perhaps we had already ignored it at our peril, as people seemed to think that Father had done, so that, whatever it was, he had left Mother with more than she could solve. On the other hand, some pursed lips and head-shaking seemed to imply, she might have done more to influence him.

It was Father's grin that I thought about, and his sudden flush when what he believed to be right was thwarted. Jem may be small, and a charmer, whereas Father upset people, but he does bring some of him to life. Mother is more elusive. I look like her but I am different. There was something in her emotions that she herself could never fulfil, although from the afternoon of the day she died I knew that I must live up to the way she behaved when the soldiers came for Father.

At the time I failed, I am afraid. Someone had sent for the women who washed and laid out the dead and I was like a deaf person: I was in the room with them but somewhere else. Then I did hear what they said, that Jem and me must not be left in the house with her, and my feelings broke, and I ran at the women and hit them and yelled.

They dragged me outside and one hit me with a wooden spoon, although where she got it from I don't know. I suppose they were already stealing things. I still shouted. Why should we leave her? Why should we leave her and the baby? You're a child they said, which made me angrier and more foolish. I blubbered and stamped.

Then Willie Ashton appeared, holding Jem by the hand, and I began to shout that Mother was dead but Jem said "I know. Mr Shorrock gave us tea in the watch-house," and as he said it I realised that it was almost dark again, and that the whole day had passed.

Father had resented young Willie because he was the master's person, and soon to be a master himself with his uncle Mr Shorrock's money, but that afternoon Willie showed his mettle. He saw that we had been angry with each other and said "What's been up, then?"

The Preacher's wife called him Mr Ashton. She had tried to keep the peace, she explained, and he said "Ask me Polly and Jem can stay here so long as your Lucy's with them." Lucy was the Preacher's eldest, engaged to be married already, and we liked her. That settled it, and we spent two nights and a day with Mother and the shrivelled baby at her side. Some people came to pay their respects, and some we knew didn't, and Jem wasn't afraid to be in the room with the bodies. In some strange way he was proud to show them to people, and I told him that if Mother's ghost did come it would be as a good spirit, to bless us; and I knew that she would want me to be strong.

"What will we do?" he said. "Who'll look after us?"

"We'll look after ourselves."

"How? How can we?"

"We've got our jobs, haven't we? We earn money, don't we?"

"Will we live in this house? Will Father come back now?"

Thinking back, I suppose that I did expect that Father would hear what had happened and would return, and that we had only to survive until he appeared. When he did Mr Shorrock would pretend that nothing had happened and take him into the mill as an overlooker, because everyone knew that Father could build and repair machinery. Another voice inside me said that Uncle Harry was owed money, that Mother had not liked Uncle Harry, and that I must be ready for anything.

Just as well. The second day saw the funeral, and Uncle Harry arrived with his wife and a lawyer. I asked what would be carved upon the gravestone, because I know that Mother had wanted a baby boy to be called William, but nobody would answer.

When we reached the field around the chapel I knew why. They were buried not in a paid-for plot but a common pauper's grave. There would be nothing of any kind to mark them. All Uncle Harry wanted was to save money, and sell everything to recover what was owed.

The lawyer asked the Preacher's wife to explain it to us. We owned nothing, it was all mortgaged and indebted.

"They can keep their clothes, I suppose," said the lawyer.

"But what about Father?" asked Jem. "He'll come for us. Won't he? Won't he come for us?"

The Preacher's wife looked around. Would nobody rescue her?

"Your Father," said Uncle Harry, "broke the law. He ran like a common criminal and knocked on my door in Manchester. 'This is the last time', I told him, 'the last money I'll ever give you.' In my opinion he ran off to America."

"America?" said Jem. "I know where that is!"

I felt unable to move, as though I'd been hit and winded. But my brain still worked and I knew, without knowing why, that Father had done some things that were brave and others that were stupid and selfish, and that even people who liked him understood why others disapproved. I saw that Uncle

Harry hated Father, and that Uncle Harry's wife looked at me with sorrow and shame, and wished that everything could have been different.

"So can we go as well?" Jem persisted. "Can me and Polly go to America?"

You can come to Manchester, they said, but there won't be any special favours. You'll work in the warehouse with the other pauper children. You'll sort cotton waste with them and earn your own keep, which will be deducted from your wages. You'll sleep and be fed in the warehouse cellar.

"There's many a well set up man," added the lawyer, "who's begun by sorting cotton waste."

I said the first thing that came into my head.

"What about Trafalgar?"

"Trafalgar?" said Uncle Harry.

"Dog," said someone.

"We can't be encumbered by a dog," said Uncle Harry. "If nobody wants him we'll have him put down."

"We want him," said Jem.

"Well you can't have him."

"For pity's sake," said the Preacher's wife, "will you leave them nothing?"

"I don't want to be uncivil, missis," said Uncle Harry, "and I respect your husband's calling, but it's none of your business and if there's a fowling piece here I'll dispatch the dog myself."

There was a fowling-piece. It was a flintlock and hung over the chimney. It had belonged to Grandfather, and it was old, rusty, and incapable of being fired with safety, but how was I to know that? Before anyone could stop me I grabbed it and ran out of the house.

Trafalgar bounced after me, and Jem, shouting "Wait! Wait for me!" We ran down the path towards the village and because we knew the muddy bits and the potholes, even in the dark, we were faster than the grown ups who chased us.

I let Jem run past me. Then I turned and pointed the gun, at which people stopped and cried out, and held up their hands as though it was loaded and I knew how to fire it.

Then off I dashed, past the mill where Grumpyguts was outside smoking a clay pipe, and looked amazed as we pelted past him. Then we were in the village, where there was all the mess and scaffolding of the New Mill being built over what had been the Town Field, and rows of cottages put up, and someone was beating a drum and another man shouting.

Who were they? Were they soldiers sent to catch us?

A daft idea, I knew, even as it came to me, but they were in long cloaks and had big hats with feathers, and the man who was shouting pointed at me and cried "Ho ho! Ho hi hum! Do my rolling orbs deceive me?"

"What?"

He took the flintlock, and with the tips of the fingers of his other hand drew mine outwards in a gesture that forced me to strike a pose. Then he surveyed me from top to toe.

I'd been stared at before, by men like Grumpyguts, but in a lip-licking sort of way when they thought I'd not noticed. That had made me shrink into myself. This was different, and confused me.

"Come on," said the man. "Embark. Over we sail to the island."

This was a wagon, I saw, on waste ground near the building works, and there was a sort of frame on it, and hangings, and steps up which he guided me. A scrunched up little man was hammering at the frame. He stopped and said "Tom? What is this? What are you doing? Who's the girl?"

"Ophelia," said Tom in the plumed hat. "Look at her. A gem. A diamond. The veritable messenger of the muse."

"Oh dear!" said the little hammerer. "Oh, dear me!"

"Say a nursery rhyme," said Tom. "Just say it."

Jem and Trafalgar stared at me, and so did the few folk drawn by the drum and display that was of course a troupe of strolling players. Well go on, said their expressions, and I knew without being told that I must stand still and pitch my voice so that the people furthest away would hear me. But not a nursery rhyme, I decided. I spoke instead the psalm that I had just heard at the funeral. The Lord is my shepherd. I shall not want.

There was silence. Then the old man cleared his throat, spat over the side of the wagon, and shouted to his wife.

"Mrs Swallow! Come over here and look at this, for you'll not see it again in your lifetime!"

CHAPTER FOUR

Such is the story of how I became an actress, invented before I could stop him by Mr Edward Wareham, and told by him to every journalist and literary person who came into the Green Room after my success with his London company. Mr Wareham told the world that he heard the story years earlier and eventually found me, the tall, strange, barefoot, dowdily-dressed and weeping apparition whom Mr Swallow had taken on at once: the orphan of the flintlock, as tittle-tattle called me, and as legend has repeated.

The truth of what happened is that it was not me but Uncle Harry who grabbed the flintlock. Alas, in his eagerness to do so he fell over and ricked his knee, which began to swell almost at once. There was swearing, cries of sympathy, and a few giggles. Uncle Harry was bulky, and flailed on the floor until someone said "You're making it worse!" At this he lay like a corpse, but with his mouth open and eyes roaming. His wife did not seem sympathetic.

Then the apothecary arrived and said "We'll have to take his breeches off," which with difficulty they did. Uncle Harry lay with his hands over his intimate parts and the apothecary looked at the knee and prodded it.

"Ow...!" yelped Uncle Harry.

"We need to try him on his feet," said the apothecary.

It was in vain. The knee would not bend, let alone take weight. The apothecary blew out breath and said "No, no, it's a job for a doctor is this."

At that time there was no doctor within miles, just as there were no lawyers, and no-one to keep order except the old parish constable. The nearest doctor was in Blackburn, and one was sent for. It was obvious that whatever the diagnosis, it would delay the removal to Manchester.

In all this to-do Jem and me had been ignored, and we went with Trafalgar to the outhouse, where we sat on the bench of the loom and Jem said "I want to go and look for Father."

"We can't do that."

"Why not?"

"We can't just set off without any idea."

"Why not?"

"Because, Jem."

"Because what?"

I was of a sudden angry again at everyone and everything, and I shook him. He hit me and I hit him back. He ran out and Trafalgar followed.

Break-neck like Father went Jem, and wouldn't stop when I shouted, so that it was because of him, and not me, that we ran down the hill. It was because Jem yelled "Leave me alone!" and ran and ran that we were brought up short by the sight of not Tom Dorchester and the drummer, but the actual performance of the play.

There was a small crowd around the wagon, and a rope enclosure within which people were expected to pay, but Trafalgar followed his nose. We ducked under the rope and wriggled our way to the front. Torches burned in the dusk and I was struck as if by an arrow. I was pierced by immediate love, as happens between two people, and although I had never seen actors before I knew that I wanted to be one.

What's more, I knew that I could do it better than the woman who was up there, not because she had a big nose and was too old for the maiden in love she was supposed to be, but because her distress did not convince me. Mother's distress had tried to hide itself but been unable to do so, and so did mine at her death, but the actress was all exaggeration.

I was bewitched nonetheless, and when it was over, when the lovers had died in each other's arms and their warring families were reconciled, when the actors had bowed and been applauded and the watchers had drifted away, me and Jem and Trafalgar remained.

We stared at the wagon which was not a wagon at all but palaces and streets and tombs. My head swam with it and when Jem spoke I did not understand.

"What?"

He pointed to where the tall young chap who had acted the doomed lover looked silly as he tried to catch a hen that scurried in front of him.

"Oh come you on!" I said, because me and Trafalgar knew how to catch hens, and without being told Trafalgar moved one way to send her the other, and into my hands, when I made the noises to soothe her.

"Very adroit!" said the young chap, who was of course Tom Dorchester. "What else can you do?"

"I'm an actress," I said.

He stood still, and looked me up and down, in the way that Father would inspect a cockerel or a cow. I was young but I thought: right! Look at me like that and I'll show you!

I began to speak and as I did so I realised that I had remembered a whole speech from the play we had seen. All of it. Without my knowing. There and then. And I felt the truth of it, as though what I said was happening to me.

I finished and Tom held out his hand to say: don't move! His eyes did not leave mine and without turning his head he cried "Mr Swallow! Mrs Swallow! Behold this!"

They came round the corner of the wagon, the trundling old scrunched up man and the woman with the big nose, and then the others. I could see that Mrs Swallow wanted to say

"What's that girl doing with our hen?" but Tom's gesture was for silence. Then he nodded and I said the speech again, after which everybody stared.

Then Mrs Swallow said "Swallow, don't stand there with your mouth open. Offer the girl an engagement."

CHAPTER FIVE

That anyone as handsome as Tom Dorchester ever stooped to trap a hen is ludicrous, I suppose, but the fact is that nothing in life is as tidy as a well-written play, or as smooth as the tales told to sell theatre seats.

"We can't simply walk off with a child," said Mr Swallow. "She might have the bosom of a family to turn to."

"We don't," said Jem

"What?"

"There you are, then," said Mrs Swallow. "It's an ill wind."

"Let it blow," said Tom Dorchester, "and don't spare the old grey horse!"

"Very characteristic of you, Mr Dorchester, if I may say so," said Mr Swallow, "but a man in my position must weigh things. This wicked uncle they describe – is he not their legal guardian? Do we want to be imprisoned for abduction?"

"We hate Uncle Harry," said Jem, "and we won't go to Manchester."

"Who are you, anyway? What's your names?"

We told him. He said "If I asked your uncle, Miss Polly, would he let you go?"

"No," said Jem

"Why not?"

"They're chapel," I said. "They've never seen actors but they think them wicked, and that they go to hell."

"Well," said Mr Swallow, "Hell contains a very big audience." He looked around to the others and said "We do all agree, I take it, that we need a juvenile tragedienne, on account of having lost the previous one in Bolton?"

"Well, I can't go on playing two different women in the same scene," said Mrs Swallow.

There were "Hear hears!" and "You carried if off well, though, don't forget that!"

Mrs Swallow gestured, in what as a grown-up woman I would call a modestly heroic way. Mr Swallow looked gloomy.

"But who says I need a cheeky boy?" he said.

For a moment Jem lost his defiance. He started to speak but nothing came.

"I won't leave Jem on his own," I said, "or Trafalgar."

"But a dog can be marvellous," said Tom Dorchester. "Dress him up and parade him when we take the town!"

"True," said Mr Swallow, "and spoken like a manager. But a boy's no use at all if he can't do six or seven jobs."

"I've got a job," retorted Jem. "I'm a bobbin boy in Shorrock's Bowling Green Mill."

"How much do they pay you?"

Jem told him. Mr Swallow winced and shook his head.

"Swallow," said Mrs Big Nose, "They're children. Stop being ridiculous."

"The best we can offer is a half share between the two of them."

I looked at Jem. He checked himself. There was an older look in his eye.

"Minus the stock debt," said Mr Swallow.

Mrs Swallow sighed, as if to say she had given up. Tom Dorchester whistled a tune to himself.

"Turn round," said Jem.

We turned our backs on the wagon.

"Are you set on this?" said Jem.

"I can do it. Can you?"

He took hold of the hen and turned back.

"What's the stock debt?" he said.

It's what the manager needs to cover expenses, explained Mr Swallow. No-one gets wages, but a profit is shared.

"I wouldn't want you to think that it's like owning one of these," he said, pointing to the mills, in which lights were coming on. We could hear machinery, and shouts from public houses, and the wind blew stink from the dye works, and from the ordure in the streets.

"One share between us," said Jem, "or I'll wring this chicken's neck."

Tom's whistling stopped. Mr Swallow's mouth fell open. Then he said "That's the spirit!" and everybody clapped and shook hands. Mr Swallow said "Hide in the wagon and keep that dog out of sight. Cover of darkness job. If anybody comes looking we'll argue, but if they don't we'll know they don't want you."

Nobody came. Tom Dorchester had a gold watch, a relic of the life he had left behind, and before first light its repeater alarm went off and we bestirred ourselves, and with the grey horse to draw the wagon and Trafalgar beside him, we stole out of town and away.

CHAPTER SIX

Mr Swallow's breakfast consisted of a raw egg broken into a mug with a splash of port wine. This would maintain the carrying power of his voice, he believed, and was the reason why his troupe travelled with a hen. At one time they had a flock of four or five, he explained as he trudged up the moor.

"What happened to them?"

"Never mind that," he said, "Next time we set up you've got to go on."

"You mean act a part?"

"How many lengths can you do?"

"Lengths?"

"Lines. How many can you learn in a day?"

I didn't know. He looked up at me. Even then he was smaller, a threadbare goblin king who pulled all sorts of faces.

"Here's the book," he said, and fished it out of his pocket. "I'll examine you this evening."

It was a scrap-book called "Romeo and Juliet," which I realised was the story we had seen the day before. Some pages were scrawled, some torn from printed volumes and stuck in, and it was written in language half of which I did not understand, but which even so made me forget that I struggled in borrowed shoes from one moorland valley to another, that snow blew in my face and that my fingers were cold.

When we were over the tops we stopped at an inn and there was a great bustle as Tom Dorchester and the drummer

Mr Edgworth donned their feathers and went ahead to take the town, as it was called: to make a stir and shout about our impending arrival and performance.

"Cheer up!" said Tom as he left, and dropped his great-coat around Jem, but the truth is that when my nose was out of the book I found it hard to do so. There was a heaviness in me, almost a nausea, at the thought of what we had done and where we were. We had run away from everything we knew. We had a few shillings from our last mill wages, but no home, no clothes and no knowledge of the life we had just joined and the people we were with. Which seems, as I stared at them in the gloomy moorland inn, to be the moment to describe them.

They were six in all. Tom Dorchester at once a friend above and beyond the others, Mr and Mrs Swallow, she being kind but clumsy and unhappy, Mr Edgworth the drummer, a pear-shaped youth who never said very much but always cut his food into very small pieces, Mr Graves and the actress Miss Witherly.

Mr Graves, older, all bones and angles and booming voice, sat now on a bench and discussed with the landlord the private habits of important persons such as the Archbishop of Canterbury and the Prime Minister. Mr Graves even knew for a fact many details about the Duke of Wellington's wine merchant. Miss Witherly plumped next to me, and said "See Mr Grave's sleeve?"

It had a hole in the elbow.

"I've offered to mend it but he refused."

"Have you known him a long time?" I said.

"Since Macclesfield. I'd walked over from Lincoln."

"Is that a long way?"

"Miles. I like your kerchief. Where's it from?"

"It was my Mother's."

"Lovely. Can I try it on?"

She snatched it from me, and wore it this way and that. Then she walked away. When we took to the road again I said "Can I have my kerchief back, please?"

"Oh, all right," she said, "If that's what you want. But we do share things, you know."

Mrs Swallow saw what had happened and made a face that said "You want to keep your eye on that one." I nodded back and lifted the book to hide my face. I won't be bested, I thought. I won't be spiteful myself but I won't be bested.

Our destination was another mill village where we were to perform the following night in a barn at the back of the inn. Tom and Mr Edgworth were there to greet us and Tom cried "Upsy daisy! I've found a fine palace for you and Jem!"

It was a loft up a ladder in the stable we would share with our grey horse Fletcher, a local donkey, Trafalgar and mice who scurried in the glow of our rush lantern. But we had sacks and straw and Jem was excited to go up and down the ladder.

"Upsy downy!" cried Tom this time. "There's a hot soup of sorts in the parlour."

We were grateful, and slurped, and said little. Mr Edgworth had a fiddle and drew approval and songs in the tobacco fug. As I warmed up I drowsed and it was a shock when Mr Swallow poked me in the arm and said "Wits about you, miss. Let's hear what you've learned."

"Here?"

"If you can't do it in this din you'll not do it on stage, will you?"

He took the book from me and opened it and said "Where from?"

"The start."

"You're not on at the start."

But I lifted my head and began.

"Wait a minute," he said. "Hold on!"

I ignored him. He listened with his mouth open. One by one the others became aware of what was happening. They seemed amazed. Then Mr Swallow snapped the book shut in front of my face, which stopped me. I've made a fool of myself, I thought. He'll scold me.

"Sorry. Have I said it all wrong?"

"You're only supposed to learn your part."

"What?"

"You've learned everything. The whole play. Everybody's lines."

"Oh," I said, and it seems to this day to be an interesting question, "is that not a good thing?"

Someone laughed, as if to say I was stupid, but Mr Swallow frowned at them and was patient with me. If I spent the next day in study, how much of my own part could I learn in time? Most of it but not all, I thought, and so it proved.

CHAPTER SEVEN

What hammering and banging and bustle as they did their best to turn the barn into a theatre: what disappointment at the clothes basket, when I went for a costume but discovered that Mrs Swallow and Miss Witherly had divided the best between them! And in any case, what remained was too big for me, so I took a man's short cloak and wrapped it around to make a skirt, and worried all the time that it would fall off. And what a beating of my heart, as I stood at the side and heard the noise of the audience, and saw the glow and shadows cast by the lanterns!

Outside the twilight was raw and cold but inside bodies packed together began to sweat, and my anticipation made it hard for me to breathe. I seemed to be rushing, and everyone else to be slow, yet I could not catch them up. Jem had his tasks and ignored me. Afterwards he said that Tom Dorchester had told him not to worry because I would do well, but I realised almost too late that the play had begun, and others were out there. They stamped and were loud to quieten the audience.

"Are the audience always noisy and silly?" I asked Tom.

"They're the instrument," he said.

"The what?"

"The instrument you'll learn to play on."

Then he shoved me because it was my turn and I stepped into what seemed like the inside of something huge and empty, except that it was filled with excitement. I carried the book so that I could use it when I reached the end of what I knew by heart, and I pretended that it was my Bible or prayer-book, or a diary in which I had pressed a flower my lover gave me. A lock of his hair I did not think that I would have, because it could betray me.

Of what passed I remember little: people's faces and gasps. Tom looking me in the eye as we acted, and the others looking into nothing and seeming unreal, neither the characters they were playing nor their true selves, whereas the onlookers were very real, and one cried "Poor soul! Poor Soul!" at my character's predicament. Then it was over and Mr Edgworth played his fiddle and some cheered and clapped and some shouted abuse, and I sat on a bench, exhausted.

Mr Swallow put his hand on my shoulder and squeezed, Mrs Swallow kissed me and Miss Witherly said "Of course you can do it! Of course you can! But then so could I in that part!"

Jem grinned and said "Close your eyes and open your mouth," and when I did he popped a pickled onion inside. I chewed it and wanted Father and Mother to have seen me. I began to cry but knew that I must not show it, and so I went to the barn and hugged Trafalgar and Fletcher and the donkey. Then I climbed the ladder and fell asleep, with the makeshift skirt still tied around me.

CHAPTER EIGHT

That we joined Mr Swallow's troupe made me and Jem grow up beyond our years, and we did so in different ways. I was a dreamer who noticed deep things as though they were not connected to me, so that their meaning would strike me much later, and explain everything. Jem trusted people less than I did. He saw into them at once, not very far but with a sense of what they were up to, and what he should do about it. We knew above all that, no matter what, with no other kin to help we must stick together, as we have to this day.

So stocky little Jem was practical. He stood a bit bandy legged with his head on one side and wanted to know how things were done: how furniture was moved, how contraptions worked, why prices went up and down and how a horse went to sleep standing up. He was quick at sums and counted the number of people in the audience. He found out who had paid and who had been given tickets in lieu of corn for Fletcher, or for victuals and lodgings, and discovered how much things cost and knew before we were told what our share would be.

I was in a threadbare fairyland, but a fairyland none the less, but Jem realised that it could not endure. We would never see Father again, he had decided, and in consequence he gave up wishful thinking.

He paid attention to all talk and emotions – and how we actors can live in hope and see the grandness in mere clouds of vapour! So Jem would hunch up and say nothing until we were out of earshot, as he did one day on the wagon in Cumberland, and said "He's skint. Mr Swallow's skint."

"Don't be silly."
"I've added it up."
"How can he be skint?"
He sulked.
"Jem!" I pleaded.
"He keeps his savings in a woollen sock."
"So?"
"There's nothing in it."
"But won't we play every night at the horse fair?"
Which we did, in a makeshift way on the wagon, with drunks shouting.
"I'm just saying, that's all. I'm just saying."
That our troupe was the poorest, and yet most ancient, form of theatre I did know, because Tom Dorchester had told me. Tom was educated and had read all the old plays. He described actors he had seen in theatres that held a thousand people, or so he said. To be ready for this I should strengthen my voice, he said.
"Ready? How will I ever that sort of chance?"
"Watch Mr Graves. He booms like a bittern but at least you can hear him. Watch how he breathes."
I did, and I asked Mr Graves as well, and he said " It's not here ..." taping his adam's apple, "... it's here ..." punching himself in the diaphragm, which in truth made him gasp, an indignity that I ignored because I began to understand.
"Time was," said Mr Graves, "time was I could whisper on stage and be heard by sandwich-board men in the street."
At this Tom would roll up his eyes, and Mr Graves foghorn on about actors in the past and how most things today were lily-livered. Tom loved old tales and led him on, and Mr Swallow would chime in, his voice low and gravelly, his lips making sunken shapes where he had lost teeth.
Mr Swallow was in a lonely place, and would mutter to himself what I knew later were old lines from Shakespeare,

and his eyes would seem to see again the actors who had mouthed them.

"Mr Kean in Hereford," he said once for no reason, "his eyes were like red-hot coals."

Before he stormed London, explained Tom when we were alone, Mr Kean had been on the road like us. Today he was ashen and drink-wrecked, and the best actor was Mr Macready.

"But I reckon that in the proper setting I could be his equal," Tom confided, "which I fully intend to attempt."

I believed him, and said so, even though when I stood next to him as we awaited our cue I often felt him tremble with the fear of having to go on at all. I did not mention this, because it would not have been tactful, but he must have seen what was in my mind because he smiled his marvellous smile and said "Yes, yes, I know about my headaches. But I can conquer London despite them!"

"I know you can," I said.

"Bravo for you, Polly Bowler!" he cried

"Polly who?"

Bowler. Because I had worked in the Bowling Green Mill, he said. I thought it a joke for the moment, and put it out of my head, not least because Jem and me agreed later that Bowling Green had been one of the mills that had put the handloom weaving out of business. As for Tom and Jem they got on well, but I sometimes thought that they did so for my sake.

CHAPTER NINE

On the last day of the horse fair it began to rain, and did not stop until we had crossed the fells and wound our way down to a fishing place on a wide estuary. When the sky cleared, clouds and sunshine played chase and shadow as far as the eye could see, and wet sands glittered. The clothes we wore, our stage clothes and our back-cloths were damp and muddy, and we spread them across thorns and boulders to dry.

We were to sleep in a run-down net store, and perform in a yard. We had two regular plays in our repertoire and everyone believed that we should prepare at least two others. Tom wanted to attempt 'Hamlet', with himself as the Prince, but Mr Swallow dithered.

"We've no playbooks," he said

"I've my own copy," said Tom. "I'll write out the parts for each person."

"We're too few in the company," said Mr Swallow, and proposed a piece that he had cobbled together himself from various old texts. He called it 'The Spanish Pirate'. There was a good part for me, he said, as the captured Princess.

"Who am I?" said Miss Witherly.

"A handmaiden."

"Humph...!" she retorted.

"We could learn it in an few days," said Mr Swallow, "and it would excite people whose livelihood was the sea."

"What d'you mean?" said Tom. "It's not Turks and Venetians again, is it?"

"It's tropical islands," said Mr Swallow.

"We gave it in Derbyshire," recalled Mr Graves, "and to very great effect."

"How long ago?" said Miss Witherly, who had come to hate handmaidens.

"What's old is what's proven," said Mr Swallow, but somehow we were downhearted, and for the first time that I saw Mrs Swallow stood out against her husband.

"We don't need discussions," she said, "not at this moment. We need to brush out these clothes and repair them."

We went back to the shore, where Jem and Trafalgar had been left on guard, and we brushed and shook and sewed and folded until Mr Edgworth cheered everybody. He and Jem had found driftwood for a fire and boiled a kettle.

As we worked the shrimpers came in with the tide, horses and carts moving slowly and girls with tucked up skirts, and baskets on their heads.

"Remember Mrs Newchurch?" said Mr Swallow.

"I kissed her," sighed Mr Graves, "not once but many times."

"Not the infamous Mrs Newchurch?" said Tom

"The very same."

"The one who – ?"

"Yes," said Mr Swallow, and Mr Graves shook his head.

"Stupid men," grinned Mrs Swallow, and they would have protested but Mr Edgworth said "The one who what?"

"Drowned," said Mr Swallow, "on more or less this very spot."

"No-one but herself to blame," said Mrs Swallow.

"What d'you mean?" said Miss Witherly.

"She dallied," said Mr Swallow.

"With a very stupid young man …" said Mrs Swallow.

"Looks, as in my case, were what consumed her," said Mr Graves, "even if he was a mere draper's assistant."

"She died for love?" gaped Mr Edgworth.

Mr Graves gestured at the horizon.

"The rest of us went on," he said. "How would she catch up? She took the short cut across the sands, and was caught up by the tide."

"Never heard of no more," said Mr Swallow, "It was her scarf that was washed up, and lay on the shore like a dead animal."

"Carlos the Dog," said Miss Witherly, very pleased with herself. "That's what she needed. Carlos the Dog."

"That attempt at humour," said Mr Graves, "was in very questionable taste."

"Fiddlesticks!" said Miss Witherly.

Trafalgar looked from one to the other and I heard myself say "Carlos the Dog?"

"Theatre Royal Drury Lane, love," said Mrs Swallow.

"Legends," said Tom, trying not to grin.

"Was the play not called 'The Caravan' ? " said Mr Graves.

"'The Caravan,'" remembered Mr Swallow.

"Regale us," said Tom. "Paint the scene."

"A dark and stormy night. A beautiful woman at the limit of grief and on a riverbank."

"Chucked herself in," said Miss Witherly. "My auntie saw it."

"She decided," reprimanded Mr Graves, "to put an end to what could no longer be endured with dignity."

"But Carlos," said Tom, "a noble creature, jumped in and saved her. Correct?"

"Correct." Said Mr Swallow.

"On stage?" I said.

"Every night!"

"Real water?"

"It was a sensation. Five hundred yard queues at the box-office."

"I suppose it was a tank," said Jem.

"It was."

"Was Carlos his real name?"

"Why is this boy so stupid?" said Miss Witherly.

"Not stupid at all," said Mr Swallow, "because if Carlos wasn't the name to which he was accustomed to respond, how could they have rehearsed him?"

"Humph...!" said Miss Witherly.

"There was unending applause," said Mr Graves. "Women wept. Strangers embraced."

"We could do this with Trafalgar," said Jem, "but I don't suppose we could afford the tank."

People chuckled. Tom's encouragement of the old men's memories had amused us. The mood was different, and Mr Swallow surprised us with his energy.

"But what we can do," he said, "is Shakespeare's 'Hamlet'!"

CHAPTER TEN

Mr Swallow's decision was to shape the rest of all our lives, but its immediate consequence was hard work. Tom made copies of 'Hamlet'. We began to learn it, and assembled as well 'The Spanish Pirate' in which I played three parts, the captured Princess and two men, a Messenger and a rascally Goldsmith, both in the same coat, but in the case of the Goldsmith with the garment worn inside-out. Even Jem had to walk on as a Barbary Ape. He did not like acting and would spoil the effect by staring at the audience to study their reactions. Then he would scratch a lot, but people seemed to expect this of an Ape, and applauded.

We were excited because we believed against all the evidence that what we were doing could transform the troupe's situation and lead to better days – days like those in the past when Mr Swallow's companies had occupied proper theatres during race weeks and Assizes. These were the days before what Mr Graves called "poor Swallow's catastrophe" although he never explained what this had been. He did teach me something, however, which was how to protect myself on stage.

Not that I asked, or that he meant to. But when I was the Princess, and he the wicked Pirate, he would grip my wrist, as though to show the audience the heat of his feelings. At the same time he twisted me, so that I faced upstage and the audience could neither see my face nor be affected by me.

Everyone was so much older than me that I did not complain. I was lucky to be there, I believed, and who cared about my troubles when they had enough of their own? At the same time I was frustrated, and I thought that to understand a scene the audience needed to see everyone. I asked Tom for advice.

Since he had been told that he could play Hamlet he was very animated. His eyes were wide, he seemed to think at twice the speed, he had no doubts about anything, and came up with all sorts of ideas.

The one that pleased us all concerned a landed gentleman named Digby Gregg, Esquire, with whom Tom had been at Harrow School. Mr Gregg's family seat was outside a market town not far from where we were on the estuary. Tom's idea was that we would rehearse, give plays along the coast, and then re-cross the fells to the market town, where he would ask his friend to bespeak some performances – that is to say, to pay our expenses in return for inviting as many people as he wished.

This had been a tradition between the gentry and strolling players, and still happened from time to time. So it became the end to which we worked. We had begun to learn the big scenes in 'Hamlet' and when I interrupted Tom to ask about my problem he was copying the last of the small parts. "What," I said, "must I do about Mr Graves?"

"Aha!" Tom cried, and pointed his quill pen at me. "So we've noticed at last! I knew we would! Bravo!"

"But what shall I do?"

He struck a pose, as though we were on the stage of a huge auditorium, and needed to be seen from hundreds of feet away.

"Survive, Polly Bowler! Survive!"

"I'm not Polly Bowler," I said.

"Oh yes you will be!" he grinned, and picked up an apple and threw it, and as I caught it he whispered "Survive!"

Which I did. I pondered, and waited until we reached

Whitehaven, which was a busy port then, with ships that crossed the Atlantic. We set up the wagon on the quay and acted in the light of flares. During our big scene together Mr Graves gripped my wrist as usual and tried to twist me, but this time I went limp. I let my head flop and my knees buckle. I fluttered to the floor in a faint.

He was shocked, thinking me ill, and released me, whereupon before he knew what I had done I was on my feet and pressed against the cloth at the back of the stage.

What would Mr Graves do? Would he turn to face me, in which case the audience would not see his face during his most important and emotional speech? Would he stand half on? Would he choose to ignore me, and speak out front?

Out front is what he risked, and hoped that he stood where he obscured me. But, of course, he could not see me, nor know what I did to make the audience laugh. When they did he turned to me, turned back, shouted his next line, and stopped.

He had forgotten where he was in the speech, I realised. I walked the few steps down to him and fed him his next line as a question.

"You never shall escape my evil clutches. Is that what you declaimed?"

He repeated the line and was secure again. We finished the scene and went off, to shouts and clapping. Mrs Swallow was poised to enter.

"Well," she said "so the kitten has claws."

On she went, blowsy, blustery and warm-hearted. Beyond her were the crowd, the lights of a tavern and the town, and at the back of the wagon the harbour. Tom Dorchester, changing from one character's nightgown into the armour of my rescuer, grinned and winked. Mr Swallow half turned from pissing over the lip of the dock into the water.

"Outrageous," he said. "Where will it end?"

"Where will what end?"

"Drury Lane if you ask us," said Tom, "with Carlos the Dog."

This made me laugh, in that gulping way of a child who had just been crying. I was half a child still, I suppose, but I deserved my own space, and was given it now, although not without sidelong glances. Mr Graves did preserve his dignity by thanking me for giving him his cue, but I still decided the next morning that I would keep a tactful distance between myself and the others, even Tom, and with Jem and Trafalgar walked twenty yards ahead of the wagon.

We were still among houses when we heard someone cry out and then a heavy thump and all sorts of other noises. Trafalgar barked and ran back and we turned, to see that Fletcher had collapsed between his shafts, the wagon come to a halt, and baskets fallen off. Trafalgar whimpered, and licked and sniffed Fletcher, but to no avail. The old horse had dropped dead, and that was that.

CHAPTER ELEVEN

It was lucky, in a grisly way, that Fletcher's heart gave out where it did, because there was a butcher in the town who bought the carcass. It would all make some sort of profit, he said: meat, horsehair for stuffing sofas, and the rest boiled down for glue. Fletcher's uncomplaining strength would exist in our memories, as it does in mine to this day. Then the wagon was sold, since Mr Swallow did not have the price of a new horse to pull it.

There were arguments about this. "Don't lose your senses," said Mrs Swallow. "Get the wagon looked after and buy another horse with your Hamlet money." Mr Swallow would not listen. "We can't rely on Hamlet," he said.

"Trust me," said Tom.

"We can't rely on money we can't predict."

"Of course we can predict," said someone, because by now they were convinced that despite Fletcher's death our luck would turn.

Mr Swallow would not budge. He entrusted one backcloth and the costume and property baskets to a carrier, and sent Tom and Mr Edgworth with them to take to town. The rest of us followed on foot, carrying what was left over. The hen we gave away, to a widow with a child in her arms.

We grumbled, but with optimism. It would be an important engagement. Strolling troupes were supposed to be licensed to perform by a magistrate, and in this case the magistrate was Tom's friend Mr Gregg. He would say "Behave with circumspection and the law will ignore you. Why put you to the cost of a licence?" Then he would pay us himself and bring people to see us. They would be quality, said Mrs Swallow, and none of your harbour riff-raff.

Tom himself, when we struggled down the fells into the market town, and found him at the lodging house that Mr Swallow had decreed was all we could afford, was edgy and excited.

"What's the matter? What's wrong?"

"This place," he said. "This place. How can we live in a flea-pit?"

He was right in that it was the worst that me and Jem had seen with the troupe. It was worse than a stable because the beds were planking and nothing provided. No candles or lamps, no covers or mattresses or headrests, which was perhaps as well because we soon began to itch. There were bugs everywhere and rats scurried. The washing place was a trough in the yard, and it faced a long doorless privy, seating holes cut in the board, that was more like a midden.

We slept together, men and women in the one room, and our fellow lodgers were drunks, beggars, discharged soldiers on the tramp and old women who had abandoned hope. Would our gear be safe here? It would not. Someone would have to guard it at all times.

Even this situation, I thought, was not the whole reason for Tom's agitation, and I was cheeky and said so.

He pulled out his famous watch, and looked at it, flicked down the cover and said "In that case, Miss Mischief, I'd better walk you out hadn't I?"

It was the end of market day, darkness falling, lanterns flaring, people still in the streets. We bought steaming hot tripe from a stall and sat on someone's window-sill to eat it. I said "Is it being Hamlet? Does that worry you?"

"Never. I could play it this minute."

He reeled off the beginning of a speech.

"Are you sure that's Hamlet?" I said, because it sounded to me like Macbeth, which I had in my bundle because he had lent it to me a few days before.

"Isn't it?" he said. "It isn't Hamlet?"

Even in this mood, and in the half-light, he looked wonderful.

"Have you got one of your headaches again?"

His dismissive shrug made it plain that he had. Oh, no, I thought. Why can't he look after himself?

"Even Jem's got more sense than you," I said.

Around us farm people were on their way home. Dogs moved a small flock of sheep.

"Jem's got enough sense for everybody," said Tom.

"An apothecary. Can't an apothecary help you?"

"The girl with all the answers," he said, with a click of his fingers, and set off.

Across the way, behind pebble-glass panes, lit by oil lamps and with a bell that jangled, there was the shop he needed. The apothecary himself was not old and scholarly, but a tall man with the energy of youth, who whistled as he worked and when he saw Tom cried "Ah! Mr Hydrographer, sir! We meet again!"

"Hydrographer?"

"He thinks I'm someone else," muttered Tom.

"A tincture?" said the apothecary, with raised eyebrows.

Tom licked his lips and wavered.

"No," he said. "Civil of you, but no. A tablet."

Small, paste-like pellets lay beneath a glass dome on the counter.

"How many grains?" said the apothecary.

"One," said Tom

"Glass of water?"

"Thank you."

The apothecary fetched it.

"Who's the real Hydrographer? How can he think you're another—?"

"Ssh ...!"

His temper surprised me. I said I was sorry. He motioned me to go outside. Through the distorting panes I saw the apothecary pick up a pellet with tweezers and drop it in Tom's palm, and Tom swallow it with a gulp of water. Then he came out and there was unease between us until he said "Damned unhappiness, Polly. Damned life that never gives us what we want. Here." He pushed a coin into my hand and said "Come on! Come and see this for a sight!"

"This" was the bustle outside the coaching inn, where the London Mail was about to set off, and it was a sight indeed: horses that were not shaggy like poor old Fletcher but groomed to gleam, the coach itself a rich chocolate colour, the Royal Arms emblazoned, the bang as the lid was locked down on the mail bags, the Guard's scarlet, his horn and blunderbuss, the snooty inside passengers, the grin of a schoolboy on top, the last rushes and tasks of others, and the other, slower, commercial coaches – the "Tally-ho" and "Thunderer" with their own eager, jingling teams: and on the box of the Mail, next to the driver, a garment that reminded me of something had been laid down to reserve a place.

There was an argument around one of the other coaches, a waiter dashed from an inn with a last-minute sandwich for someone, the driver of the Mail drained a mug of porter and threw the mug back to a maid. The church clock struck the half-hour.

"On the King's service, gentlemen!" yelled the Mail driver, and as he snapped off the brake, and the Guard blew his horn, Tom Dorchester swung up on to the box beside him, threw into my arms the cloak from our Costume Basket that had marked his place, and the coach clattered over the cobbles and away.

CHAPTER TWELVE

Was it stage fright? Was pure and simple stage fright the reason why Tom ran away, or was there more? Was it an impulse? How could it have been, if our property cloak lay on the box of the London Mail? He must have paid an ostler to put the cloak next to the driver, or the driver himself to keep the place. For how long this had been planned? In the flicker of a miserable wick in tallow the company was awake half the night, and asked but could not answer these questions. Above all, what would happen now to our bespoke performances?

Had Tom even spoken to his school friend Mr Gregg, asked someone. If we did perform what play would it be? Without the prince we could not do 'Hamlet', but we could patch or double up parts in other plays, We could be the masters of our fate. Of course we could, and even ran through words and tried out scenes there and then, until other lodgers in the house yelled at us to stop.

When we snuffed out the light I felt the fear that is like a loose stomach, and weakens all one's muscles. Jem clung to me like a toddler again, and like the others, we pretended to fall asleep but could not. Tomorrow, I thought, would reveal the worst.

Tom's school friend Mr Gregg was to preside over the Magistrate's Court, we knew, and it had been arranged that Tom would take Mr Swallow to meet him. Now he must go alone, without Tom, and there was a great fuss over brushing his clothes, and sending him to a barber for a shave.

Mr Swallow wanted to save his money but the women said "Don't be ridiculous." When he sighed they added "You can't look as though you've slept in a place like this, even when you have."

"I suppose I smell of it," he said.

"Have the barber do a dash of cologne."

Mr Graves started a discussion about pomades and shaving oils, absurd in the circumstances of our eating breakfast outside a pie-shop, but it was a distraction, and seemed to assert that in fact we were persons of distinction, and above all this.

Mr Edgworth had been left with Trafalgar as watch dog and we took them sausages in a paper twist. Then Mr Swallow appeared, shaved and tidied, and made one of his decisions. He told me to change into the white dress I wore in the last scene of 'The Spanish Pirate', which Mrs Swallow kept washed and flat-ironed when she could.

She protested now that it was clean but crumpled, and that she should be the one to accompany Mr Swallow, but he said "No. Just throw a sash around it." She continued to argue but he stopped her.

"A pretty girl can make a difference," he said. "It can make a man see what depends on it."

"Nothing depends on it," she said. "Not from his point of view. Can you not see that?"

Mr Swallow had shepherded his flock for so long that no, he could not see other points of view, so that as we sat in the courthouse corridor he patted my hand and said,

"Don't worry. Worse things happen at sea, and I've survived them."

There were shouts and commotions from the cells. Last night's drunks were let out, and a sheep-stealer shoved in, to await his transfer to the Assizes. Then the session seemed to be over, but nobody came for us. When a Constable passed Mr Swallow asked if our message had been delivered, but "Nowt to do with me," was the reply.

Even the cells were silent. Had everyone gone home? How small I felt, and untidy despite the dress, and not sure that I was pretty, nor of how to make a difference. Then a young man popped his head out of a door and said "Swallow?"

"Yes."

"Well, come on. What are you waiting for?"

The Magistrate's Room had panelling, a stone floor and a merry fire burning, and Mr Gregg himself was fresh-faced and corpulent, in shirt sleeves and stockinged feet. He had a napkin tucked into his collar band, and a small hawk perched on his desk amid papers and dirty plates. With a tin fork Mr Greg fed him what was left of a cold chop.

"Ah, there you are," he said. "No point in giving you a licence. Haven't seen strolling players for years. Didn't know there still were any. Just give your show, keep quiet, and bugger off, I'd say." Mr Swallow wanted to explain but was waved silent.

"No need for thanks. Have a mug of ale to seal it. What about your daughter? Anthony," he said to his servant, "find the young lady a biscuit."

"She's not my daughter," said Mr Swallow.

"What?"

"It's about Thomas Dorchester," said Mr Swallow.

"Dorchester? What's he to do with you?"

For the first time Mr Swallow faced the extent of our troubles. For one obvious thing, Mr Gregg was much too old to have been Tom's schoolfellow.

Mr Swallow started to explain.

"He what?"

"He thought that you'd bespeak the performances."

"You mean he's an actor?"

The servant Anthony, biscuit barrel in hand, wanted to speak.

"What?" said Mr Gregg.

"Your Mother, sir," said Anthony. "If you recall."

"Thank you," said Mr Gregg, as it dawned on him. "I do. I'm afraid I do."

He took care as he gave the hawk the last piece of meat. The bird's black and yellow eyes were hard and pure, like gemstones.

"Mr Dorchester was a sometime acquaintance of my younger brother," said Mr Gregg.

"Ah, well. Then happen it was your brother who—"

A hand still holding the fork stopped him.

"No such luck. My brother's with his regiment. In Gibraltar."

"Oh."

"Yes."

Mr Swallow struggled to recover hope.

"Are you a follower of the dramatic arts yourself, sir?" he said.

"No, no. Playing cards for me, Mr Swallow. And the outdoors. And pedigrees, you know. Mother has a keyboard of course."

Even at this Mr Swallow stirred, but saw that it was useless.

"I'm sorry, then," he said. "A misunderstanding."

Mr Gregg untucked his napkin. He was direct.

"I've no sympathy for Mr Dorchester myself, you understand. I told Anthony to send him away. But he persisted, I believe?"

"He did," said Anthony, and pursed his lips.

"You'd better tell Mr Swallow what happened."

"Your Mother never lends money if there's no hope of return, sir, but she did give Mr Dorchester more than enough to see him to London."

Mr Swallow managed to ask the questions.

"Did he – Well, begging your pardon, but did he say why he needed to go?"

"To get away from all this, and save what he could."

"All this?" said Mr Swallow, and I thought: to save what he could? Poor Tom. How confused he must be. Yet there is always good in him.

Mr Gregg belched, patted his chest, took a swig from his half-tankard, and stood up. Mr Swallow nudged me to do the same. The hawk fluttered and settled again.

"There we are," said Mr Gregg. "If only things were different. But there we are."

Mr Swallow made a sweeping, out-of- date farewell bow, like a courtier in an old play, and we left the room.

CHAPTER THIRTEEN

The coin that Tom had given me was a golden guinea but I did not tell anyone, not even Jem, because when I tried to explain about Tom's headaches and the apothecary Miss Witherly had said, "Oh, yes, we all know what that means!" and everyone ignored or talked over me. I did not know what it meant, and decided to keep quiet in the hope that I might hear, but all they talked about was themselves. It was the same when Mr Swallow recounted what the magistrate had said.

He spoke as though there was little to worry about. Performances might be given and money recouped, he said, but no-one believed him. Mistrust and selfishness went like an infection from person to person, and Mrs Swallow blamed and accused him.

He had never listened to her, she said, never done what was best, and what's more he had broken his promise to marry her: because he was a liar and married already, she shouted, to that ridiculous woman who thought she was the Queen of Yorkshire – at which Mr Swallow tried to protest but was yelled down – and anyway the fact was that both Mrs Swallow and Miss Witherly had their careers to think of, as she put it. She demanded that the company be disbanded, and that what money remained be shared out.

She no longer loves him, I realised. She wants to get out, and she's found the excuse. Mr Swallow himself seemed weary, and to have shrunk, and for the first time I realised that he was decades older than her. I should always have seen that, I thought, and yet that's how we grow up, isn't it, through discoveries of our own ignorance?

Mr Swallow did not want to fight back in public. A quarrel between the two of them, he said, did not concern the other actors, nor the company itself. It was not for Mrs Swallow to put other people's lives at risk. She could at least have waited until the end of the season.

"Season? What season? You call losing money in shit-holes a season?"

This was not about her and him, repeated Mr Swallow, it was about everybody.

But everybody had gone outside. They were embarrassed and did not want to listen, not even Miss Witherly. Jem and I were furthest from the door and stayed in the corner because we did not want to draw attention to ourselves; and it was our existence, after all, that was being argued about by other people, and we wanted to know what was said.

In a play, or at least a well-written one, things happen in order, but here it went on for hours, to and fro, coming and going, deciding this and then choosing the opposite, stamping in frustration or sitting in silence for minutes on end.

Then a new argument would start, that was not to the point, or Mr Swallow would repeat that we were the servants of the public and theatre our calling. We must take the bad with the good. At this Mrs Swallow would return to the money and how much was left.

"It's not about the money!" he complained, but it was, as it most times is, I have discovered.

"Put it to the vote! Put it to the vote!" insisted Mrs Swallow, because the company had votes according to its shares. But Mr Swallow would not, because he knew that, as it proved, they were against him.

"What about our vote?" piped Jem, but someone said "Don't be ridiculous!" and by now Mr Swallow was too tired to resist. There was no vote as such, because to keep some dignity he decided himself to pull the old sock from his pocket and count out what there was.

"What about this junk?" said Mrs Swallow, meaning the scenery and costumes and props, that were piled around the room. They picked over it like gulls on a rubbish dump until Mr Graves said, " In all conscience and tradition this does belong to the Manager." So they stopped, but kept what items they could carry.

On an impulse Mr Swallow said, "Mr Edgworth. You've been tolerably civil. Why don't you keep the drum?"

"Thank you," said Mr Edgworth. "Thank you very much."

However hard he tried Mr Edgworth's voice and expressions were comical, so that he could act servants, and people amazed by what happened, but nobody serious. Now he festooned himself with the drum, his bundle, the fiddle and his second overcoat, and shook hands with each of us.

"I think I'll make for my auntie's in Liverpool," he said, and clattered out.

Nobody spoke. Then with a lot of noise Mr Edgworth reappeared.

"Sorry," he said. "Forgot the drumsticks."

His second departure left a longer silence. We might never see him again, we realised. Then somebody said "Phew..!" as though the air was cleared. But it was not, because Mrs Swallow would not stop her complaints.

They made my head ache, as Tom's had ached, and I nudged Jem to come outside.

"Do you hate this as much as me?" he said. "What must we do?"

"Stay with Mr Swallow."

"Why?"

"If we don't we'll feel bad."

He signed and scuffed his feet.

"Is an actress still what you want to be?" he said.

51

"More than ever. But I can't feel bad about things, Jem."

He studied me.

"If I'm bad, how can I act people who are good?" I said.

"What about Mr Edgworth?" he said.

"What?"

"He wasn't funny to himself, was he? People just saw him as funny."

This is very interesting, I thought, but we can't discuss it now.

"Jem: yes or no? Should we be loyal to Mr Swallow?"

"Of course we should," he said. "Anyway, I want to be like him."

"You what?"

"A manager. You know."

"No."

"The one who manages it all."

This time I studied him.

"They all think it's them," he said, "but the manager knows it's him."

Cocky little sod, I thought.

"I'll be your manager," he said. "You've got the magic."

"Don't be silly."

"There's plenty of time," he said. "Years and years and years."

"Yes. But what about tomorrow?"

"I know," he agreed. "And suppose Mr Swallow doesn't want us?"

"In that case," I said, "we'll have to have another think."

Jem nodded. The yard stunk of the privy but there was clean country beyond, and beyond that a red and yellow sky. They've argued for hours, I thought, and now it's day's end, and they must stay until morning.

CHAPTER FOURTEEN

But I was wrong. They disliked their situation so much that they spent more than they could afford on southbound stage-coaches and carriers' carts, and Mr Swallow sat alone amid the wreckage. He had donned his big coat with the shoulder flaps and in the shadows looked like one more pile of clothes on top of the rest. He looked at me through watery eyes and named a sum of money.

"It's what you're owed. If you want to go take it, but it won't get you far, God help you."

"We want to stay," said Jem.

"What?"

"Until you release us," I said.

"You're children," he said. "Are you bloody mad?"

We felt forlorn. "How can this be happening?" he said. "Don't you realise I've only one place left to go?"

"Where's that?" said Jem, in a tone that feared it might be somewhere very bad indeed.

"Queen of Yorkshire," said Mr Swallow. "A nemesis and overwhelming fate."

We stared at him. What was a nemesis? Words failed us.

"The worst of it is," he continued, "that it's what she always prophesied!"

He mumbled, gestured to himself, blew his nose, started to speak, stopped, shook his head and scrutinised us.

"I reckon I thought you'd gone," he said, "but here you are. So what's to be done about you?"

"Don't worry about that," said Jem. "Just teach us what you can while you can."

This pleased Mr Swallow. He leant forward and lowered his voice.

"First lesson, " he said. "All things must pass. Ozymandias King of Kings. Look what happened to Napoleon Bonaparte. What's that line from Shakespeare? I can't remember. I've been shaky on words for a year or two. Did anyone notice?"

"Never," I said, although more than one I had been acting with him when he had gone blank but rescued himself with words from another character or even another play.

His glance was keener. He knew, I saw, that to be tactful I had lied.

"Quite right, Miss Polly," he said. "It's a poser is that one. Sometimes the truth's best and sometimes it isn't."

"I'll remember," I said.

"Promise?"

"Promise."

"And another thing," he said, "even after Waterloo, Bonaparte must have needed a cheese pie, mustn't he?"

"What's a nemesis?" said Jem, "and who was Ozymandias King of Kings?"

"I'll explain on the way," said Mr Swallow.

"But what about all this?"

Jem meant the piles of the company's stuff that remained.

"Leave it. Just bring your own bundles."

In the street he wobbled more and leaned on me for balance. "Your nemesis, " he said, "is what does for you in the end, and as often as not you've deserved it."

"You mean like Tom Dorchester?" said Jem. "Was he a nemesis?"

"May be he was, but there was something about him that's beneath discussion, so we won't."

Unfair I thought, and recalled Tom's looks and ambitions and dash. But I did not say it, and as we sat on the rim of a horse-trough and ate our pies Mr Swallow confessed that he had no idea who Ozymandias was, but thought that it was a mighty poetic line that stirred the soul.

"Give us another," said Jem.

Mr Swallow struck a pose and cried "Is it not passing fair to ride in triumph though Persepolis?" and as if summoned by him the Manchester Mail clattered past, the Guard blowing his horn and dogs barking alongside.

For that magical moment the town became an ancient city, its few dull lights the lanterns of bazaars, but when we returned to the lodging house half the stuff we left had been stolen, as Jem had feared it would be.

Mr Swallow was unperturbed. He even sniffed with satisfaction and said "That's a lot less to get rid of, then, isn't it?"

He had asked at the pie shop where the boneyard was and in the morning men came with a cart to take away what was left: the torn back-cloths, the paper collars with ink-spots to imitate ermine, the mop-sticks painted like swords, the broken baskets, the old box full of stones that used to be shaken to sound like thunder, and the collars worn by the horses.

"Poor old Beaumont," sighed Mr Swallow, "and poor old Fletcher ..."

He retained some play books, and gave me an old military waistcoat that he said might do for Trafalgar in cold weather, as indeed it still does, although of course there are no holes for his back legs to go through.

Mr Swallow had managed not to be bitter, but to give up the struggle as well as his stock goods, and if his limbs were creakier because he no longer needed to pretend to be imposing, his spirits were lighter. This was an extraordinary sight because most people do not want to be discarded, and stripped of their use and dignity.

But for several days we wandered around the little town,

and when we were pointed out as the ruined actors, Mr Swallow would raise his hat and tell anyone who would listen how happy he was. It had been like the Great Fire of London, he said. What he owned had been consumed by the flames, but he was alive, and as merry as a chorus of throstles. Throstles, I thought, singing away in the mill. Mr Swallow's listeners assumed that we were his grandchildren, and we did not deny it.

For Jem and me these days were very strange. Would Mr Swallow release us? Did he think he needed us? What would he do if he was alone? Why didn't he set off for Yorkshire? What if his money ran out? Most old people went to the poorhouse, we knew, but many died in the street, or in fields or outhouses. Mr Swallow told everyone that he was part of theatrical history, which was all that mattered. Stars flash across the sky, he proclaimed, and the rest is oblivion.

"Do you think he's mad?" asked Jem.

"I don't know."

"Wait and see, then?"

"Yes."

After supper Mr Swallow allowed himself a tot of rum, and gave Jem and me a splash of it in our mugs of hot water, and in the tallow light we read scenes from the old play scripts. Other lodgers did not complain but crept near to listen, and they were the owls in the Forest of Arden, the nightjars in Mr Shakespeare's dream woods, and flitted away when we finished. Mr Swallow would lurch back from the privy, and a cough and a spit in the yard, and one night he said "Do you two know why I've waited?"

"No," I said.

"To pluck up courage," he said.

"What for?"

"To go home," said Mr Swallow. "Four walls and a roof."

He had a home? He had a house? He had more than the

hard boards of wagons, and summer hedge bottoms, all manner of inns and these last, damp, verminous and peeling quarters?

But we said nothing. We were shivery. What did this mean for us?

"If you help me on my way," said Mr Swallow, "I'll do my best to see you right at the end."

CHAPTER FIFTEEN

Mr Swallow reckoned that it would take us three or four days to walk across the Pennine moors – the roof of England, he called it – and through sweeter country to the ancient city of York. What he had miscalculated, or perhaps ignored, was the extent to which his health had worsened. His breath was shorter and his knees weaker. There were a few stretches of easier walking on the turnpikes, but most of the way was pack-pony trails, greasy with mud in the wet, rutted and stony in the dry.

For Jem and me it was exciting to see the high hawks and the panoramas, and for Trafalgar to make game birds clatter up and bound after them, but Mr Swallow looked nowhere but at the difficult ground in front of him. Once he fell and must have been in pain, but he insisted he was not.

Twice we found lodgings and poor suppers in drovers' inns, but after we had travelled in three days the distance we should have covered is less than two, darkness and rain caught us early, and we had to sleep in the lee of a sheepfold.

Mr Swallow would talk when we stopped, rambling memories that made more sense to me later than at the time, and he described the bookseller we would meet in York, the printing press at the back of the shop, and the walk through the alleys to the stage-door of the theatre. It seemed to be important to learn this route, although he did not explain why, and he seemed not to have acted in the theatre itself, not even when it was a different building on a different street, and before Mr Whatshisname was the manager.

Mr Whatshisname and his wife Mrs Whatshername I had

heard discussed by the company, and they were talented, ungenerous, handsome or uninteresting according to who spoke of them. I wanted Mr Swallow to be precise about them but he hemmed and hawed and muttered about money owed, as if that was what hurt the most, he said. The bookseller knew about poets, he said, but I should always pay the most attention to Mrs Whatshername.

"Time was!" he said. "Time was! Oh dear, Miss Polly. Dear, dear me..."

On the fourth day, although we were in a grubby state, he had more energy and his eyes blazed more, but it was a false promise. His tiredness made us stop and sleep once again in the open, yet by the next afternoon we were over the top, and descended with a little river a long valley of the dales.

Ahead of us there were houses and a church amid trees. A cold sun came out. Mr Swallow stopped and said "What's taken place, Polly? Why is it dark of a sudden?"

He leaned on me, lowered himself to this knees, and then to all fours. His neck hung down. Trafalgar sniffed and whimpered. Mr Swallow had a pack on his back and tried to get it off, but could not. He rolled to one side under its weight. I gestured at the houses ahead and Jem went for help. Trafalgar started to run with him, but turned back to be near Mr Swallow, who said, "Tell me some Shakespeare, Polly. What can you remember?"

I could remember whole plays, and although the air was cold and I began to shiver, and saw that spring snow was blowing, and the sun making the flakes glint, I spoke all the parts as well as I could. I had reached the first meeting of the lovers when Jem returned with a clergyman and some others. They lifted Mr Swallow and carried him, half-dropping him once it must be said.

CHAPTER SIXTEEN

The clergyman asked my name and what we were, and introduced himself as Mr Eaton. He was well-spoken but nervous as well as serious, and found it hard to look me in the eye. When he could, it was with a sort of pleading directness.

His parish was that of High Pockstones, he said, and what was Mr Swallow's persuasion, did I know? "No," I said. "What about yourself?" he said.

"Chapel," I said, which we were, against the Government, Father had said, and against all who seek to dictate conscience.

Mr Eaton smiled and said "Well, so are most of my theoretical parishioners, I fear." Which they were, we discovered, and even held meetings on the moors, singing wildly, and shouting revelations out loud, while young Mr Eaton read the King James Bible to a near-empty church.

At the back of his rectory there was a yard and horses looked with interest from their loose boxes as Mr Swallow was lugged past them to the bakehouse and laid upon a table. There was retained warmth from the oven and a small intense woman had arrived to take charge. She resembled Mr Eaton but was a year or two older. She had lost teeth and chewed her lip, and a sprig of rosemary was pinned to the shawl across her sombre clothes.

"Who are they Robert?" she said. "Where are they from? What have you discovered?"

"Theatricals," said Mr Eaton.

"God help us," she said. She was his sister, I guessed, as she did not have a wedding ring.

"Should we send for the doctor?" she said. "How long would that take?"

"Two hours."

"Who'd pay?"

"He's got money," said Jem. "An old sock in his pocket."

"Come here child," said Miss Eaton. "I must look at you."

Jem stood foursquare in front of her. She ruffled his hair and peered.

"Just as I expected," she said, and beckoned me.

I resented it but went to her, whereupon she inspected my head as well.

Mr Swallow had come around, I realised, and tried to struggle, and to speak in a slurred voice. I wanted to help the men who calmed him but Miss Eaton said "No, no. This is providential. God has sent us a family. But next to God is cleanliness. You've got lice, do you know that?"

I suppose I did, but pretended not. We all knew what had infested that dismal lodging house, and I had seen Jem itch, but I was in such mixture of misery and hope that I ignored my own discomforts.

"Bertha!" Miss Eaton shouted. "Hot water! Vinegar! Scissors! New Clothes! Come on!"

That I was disgusted at my own filthiness is the reason I went with meekness to the wash-house and the humiliations: stripped naked, our clothes taken away to be burned, ourselves stood in a trough, scrubbed, scraped, doused in vinegar and, worst of all, our hair hacked off.

Even clean, and in new clothes, I felt naked.

CHAPTER SEVENTEEN

Where had these clothes come from? Whose were they? I was in the unlikely garments of the sort of child I had never been, nor ever expected or now wanted to be: the frilly pantaloons, the flouncy dress held at the waist with a sash-ribbon, and a shawl to sit upon my shoulders. Not a sturdy mill-girl shawl to defy rain and snow, but a silly spun-sugar confection to admonish the draughts that come around drawing-room doors. I should have felt magical in such a thing, and in their grown-up equivalents I do, but my hair was a mess of tufts and bug bites showed on my arms and neck. Jem was in corduroys and a smock that was too large for him.

We wanted to see Mr Swallow but Bertha bustled us into the kitchen and plonked us on a settle. "Are they vermin free?"

"Squashed 'em all," said Bertha. "Forefinger and thumb. Squeezed every one to pieces."

"What's on the stove?"

"Rabbit stew."

"Feed them, I think."

Mr Eaton came in. He began to explain something but stopped when he saw us. His sister was alert.

"Writing materials," he said.

He made to enter the house proper but stopped when he realised how we had been sheared, and were dressed. He seemed not to approve, but said nothing, fetched a writing box, and returned to the outhouses.

Jem asked about Mr Swallow but was told to eat what was

put in front of him. Even this kitchen, I saw, contained more good things than any other place we had known, although I spotted that Miss Eaton's clothes were old and mended with great skill.

They had lit lamps now and a range fire roared and despite our unease we felt snug. Did we snooze for a while? I am not sure, but it was dark when the latch clattered and one of the men was on the threshold. He indicated that we should follow, to where in lantern flickers and shadows Mr Swallow lay with his boots and most of his clothes off, and a blanket over him.

His eyes were closed. His breath came in rasps. Mr Eaton indicated that Miss Eaton should sign a paper that lay on the open flap of the writing box. She did so. Bertha and the men looked very solemn. Then Bertha began to sing, and the men joined in. Bright morning star, oh my soul, oh my soul. Mr Eaton's lips moved soundlessly as he read the prayer book.

Then he stopped and looked, and so did the others, and in the silence we realised that Mr Swallow was dead.

"Amen," said Miss Eaton. "That blanket must be burned."

Amen. Amen and amazed looks at her. Some of the ink on the paper gleamed still, and Mr Eaton shook sand across it. Jem gripped my hand.

CHAPTER EIGHTEEN

How long does it take hair to grow back? Mine returned by about an inch a month, so for a long time I did not wish to see myself, or others to see me, without a mob cap. Once in Bowling Green Mill I had seen a woman catch her hair in the machinery. She was dragged down and her face mashed, and when the machine was stopped had to be cut free of it. But even when she returned to work, with her looks spoiled forever, she would not wear a cap or head-tie.

A woman's hair is her self and her glory, and how she dresses it a sign of many things. Mother's hair was long. For chapel she pinned it up inside a bonnet, and in the house where she was mistress wore it loose. But she held it in a tie at the loom, or when people came.

This was bold, I now know. Girls wore long hair, and mine had come almost to my waist, but married women put theirs up, to show that they belonged to someone. Mother loved Father and Jem and me but most of her belonged to no-one but herself, unlike Miss Eaton, who belonged to no-one at all. Miss Eaton's hair was as tightly-packed and held down as on most days she tried to keep her feelings. On others they would not stay in place.

Once she brought from the attic and had us erect the toy theatre of her childhood, and said that she had been taken to the real theatre to see Mr Kean play King Richard the Third. He had frightened her. His eyes had flashed and his hair had been all over the place.

"How long will it take Polly's hair to grow?" said Jem.

Long hair, she said, is not shown by ladies, but by drabs in public houses, by the likes of actresses and artists' models, and by much, much worse.

"Worse? Who's worse? What's worse?"

"May you never discover," she said.

"But Polly's an actress," he retorted.

"Not any more."

"She's an actress and this is a toy theatre."

"You're a very impertinent boy," she said. "Stand in the corner."

Which he did, because he knew the choices we faced. We had not been rounded up and sent to a mine or a factory, as we knew street children were, nor sent to a poorhouse, nor kept as skivvies and beaten if we tried to run away. Not that we had anywhere to run, except to a bookseller and a theatre we did not know, and where common sense told me not to go at all until my hair was grown and I myself again, and able to show what I could do.

No, we had been deloused, dressed, fed and sent to bed early as though we were real rectory children. We had an attic room next to Bertha. It was called the Nursery, and we had a bed each, old toys, rugs on the floor, texts on the wall, a shelf of improving books, a wash-stand and chamber-pot, and a chest full of clothes, some for grown-ups, some moth-eaten, some mended with infinite and detailed love.

There was a room in the outbuildings called The Schoolhouse, where other children came twice a week for lessons from Miss Eaton and the rector himself. They were the boys and girls of the better off yeomen, and a shopkeeper and a wheelwright. But with most of the village children we were not supposed to play, because they were said to be violent and common.

One of Mr Eaton's classes was called the Kings and Queens of England: Alfred and the cakes, Harold with the arrow in his eye at Hastings, Good Queen Bess who saved us from the Spanish, William who come from Orange to save us from the Irish and old King George who went mad but saved us from the French. All these foreigners would have taken away our liberty, said Mr Eaton, the best defenders of which were the King, the constitution, and the Church of England.

Mr Eaton was against more people being given the vote. In his opinion we had all the liberty we need and persons such as himself would protect us. It was made clear that an example of this was the way in which he took strays like Jem and me into this own home, to give us a second chance. But according to Tommy Tapper, our best friend in the schoolroom, there had been two or three before us, and because they had behaved badly, or the rector and Miss Eaton disagreed, they had been sent to work in factories in Leeds.

We were never sure who was on our side or who was not, but we knew that Mr Eaton and his sister argued about us, because we overheard them.

"They are not our children and they are not our family."

"They could have been," she protested.

"No they could not."

"They could have been my own—"

"I beg you not to shout!"

Silence. My own breath. Then her feet on the boards and the rustle of her skirts.

"Don't touch me. Do not touch me!" he said in a whisper.

"Is it my fault?" she hissed. "Is the fault mine?"

"No."

Then Jem blundered along and they knew we were there. I knocked on the lintel and said "May we look at the atlases, please?" I did know what an opportunity the books presented, and that Mr Eaton wanted me to seize it.

Another time I heard their voices raised and Mr Eaton

shout "In God's name, I am bound by a man's dying wishes!"

"What isn't known can't hurt, though, can it?"

"What am I to think you mean by that?"

"My feelings need time," she replied. "I need time, Can't you see that I burn like a furnace?"

Was this to do with Mr Swallow? Was it to do with me and Jem? Where could I find answers to what I asked myself about Miss Eaton? One day, I decided that simplest is best. I was helping Bertha to make bread and said "Why has Miss Eaton never married?"

Bertha stopped, her hands in the dough. Then she said "Too poor, aren't they? Him and her. Church mice."

Too poor? How can they be poor when they have curtains and family pictures and comfortable chairs and books and Bertha and a girl who comes in from the village, and money over to run the school? Mr Eaton had been to Oxford University, and he rode to hounds, and they both went out with fowling-pieces and shot for our suppers, and sometimes other clergymen would come to dine, as would Henry Hall, who trained Lord Markenfield's racehorses. How could such people be poor?

"Poor in their world, love," said Bertha, "not in ours." And she added "Lord Markenfield's poor. Can't come home, can he? Spends his time in German watering places."

"What's a watering place?" said Jem.

"It's where they drink them health salts and gamble," said Bertha.

"Right," said Jem, who knew Markenfield's jockeys, and would go to the stables, to help muck out and even ride work, sometimes. He was after all very small.

"Tommy Tapper says that his Mother's cousin's wife heard someone on market day say that Miss Eaton had been proposed to, but left in the lurch. Would that be because he discovered she'd no money?" I said.

"I know Tommy Tapper's Mother's cousin's wife," replied Bertha, "and she's what I'd call a tittle-tattle."

I had more questions, but something in Bertha's stare, as she nodded for me to add water to the dough, warned me to desist.

CHAPTER NINETEEN

Emotions flared most days between Miss Eaton and her brother, and with me and Jem she could be nasty, in the name of a common sense that would have been admirable but for the fact that it was crazy. Accomplishments which she strove to induce in me included needlework, dressmaking, the pianoforte, sketching from nature, deportment, the correct laying of cutlery, forms of address, and the reading of postal library novels that might provide a topic with which to maintain a conversation at a dinner party.

They have all been of eventual use to me in one way or another, but that they would enable Miss Eaton to chaperone me to York, or to a spa like Harrogate, and find me a suitable husband was as deluded a notion as her insistence that Jem could at the age of thirteen or so attend a school like Rugby or Harrow: to finish him off, as she put it, and enable him to make friends with important people.

These ideas would be broached at the lunch table, when Mr Eaton would sink his chin upon his chest and not speak, whereupon she would flare up about some other subject. Mr Eaton would not be provoked and in the silence Jem would say "But at the stables I do meet important people," which in its way turned out to be true, although at the time Miss Eaton would say "Don't be ridiculous. And don't slouch. Sit correctly."

Ridiculous and correct or whatever, it was the horse-racing that broke the spell. Seasons had passed and Jem had chattered about handicaps for weeks but we did not listen. Then one afternoon he returned from the stables with Henry Hall himself, and Mr Eaton broke off from whatever it was they discussed to call "Polly. Will you attend us in my study?"

Mr Hall was a big, sweaty, swearing untidy man with shrewd squinty eyes and a grin. Jem was trying not to burst with excitement, I could see, and Mr Eaton said "There seems to be a horse called Cloudy Mary."

"We think she's a chance," said Mr Hall, "especially if Trafalgar and Jumping Jem go with her."

"Go with her? Who's 'Jumping Jem?' Another dog?"

"Your brother here, it seems," said Mr Eaton.

"Oh."

I felt silly and blushed.

"Some horses," expanded Mr Hall, "need their families around them, or else it's fits and smelling salts time."

"Oh," I repeated, and realised that Jem had rolled his eyes up in that way men do at what they consider to be a female's inability to understand what's important.

"It seems that Rainy – I apologise – Cloudy Mary warms to Trafalgar in particular," said Mr Eaton.

"We've got the money on," emphasised Mr Hall. "Every advantage must be squeezed."

Outside was breezy sunlight, but in the room the drugged stuffiness of curtains, carpets and huge book-cases, and in the grate a fire smouldered. The men seemed so much bigger and more ponderous than me. I looked at both of them and said "Very good. But where do I come in?"

Jem seemed to wriggle about inside his clothes. He's letting us down, I thought, and frowned at him.

Mr Hall laughed and said "Bless my belly, but we need Jem and Trafalgar at the races, and if you'd join us, Miss Hindle, we'd be very obliged."

Miss Hindle was me, I realised, and gave a nervous nod.

"Come on, Jem," said Mr Hall, "help me saddle up again."

Off they went. It was an excuse, I thought, to leave me and Mr Eaton together.

I looked at Mr Eaton. He was staring at my hair and there was embarrassment. He had touched me sometimes, on my arm or shoulder or cheek, but jerked away in the instant. I wanted to leave.

"What I must confess, Polly," he said, with a gesture to detain me, and speech that seemed to come as a relief, "is that Mr Swallow made me his Executor to act when I saw fit, and I—"

He waved his hand, as if to make the intervening months disappear.

"He left very little money, I fear – because as you know he desired a proper funeral and headstone."

"I don't need money," I blurted. "I've got Tom Dorchester's guinea."

"What?"

"Outside the apothecary's. He gave me a guinea."

This was more that he could deal with at the moment.

"And we've sixteen shillings and four pence halfpenny as what's left of our share."

"Polly, I must insist that you listen. As well as his will, Mr Swallow was able to dictate a letter, and have me seal it. It was for you. To take to someone in the theatre."

"Mrs Whatshername?"

"Do you know her?"

"Not yet."

"Is your hair – I mean – Are you ready? Is the length sufficient?"

"Yes."

Just about, I thought. And before I could stop myself I spun around on tip-toe with my skirts held out, and faced him again.

He smiled, which he did not do very often.

"You know, I presume, that the actors perform during race-week, so that you could deliver your letter?"

"Yes."

He nodded. "Do you have any lodgings in mind?"

"The booksellers pro tem, Mr Swallow said."

"Pro tem."

"Yes."

"I love to read plays," he said, "but I cannot say that I approve of theatrical life."

It's better that the coal mines or Bowling Green Mill, I thought.

"But I made a promise to Mr Swallow, whose respect for you I recognised, and I think that I must keep it. We sheltered others before you, and no doubt others will follow."

He seemed uneasy. I looked him in the eye.

"What about Miss Eaton?" I said.

"She will pray for you of course," he said. "For the present, she has retired to her room with a most severe lassitude. It will afflict her for days, until I exorcise it."

CHAPTER TWENTY

In those days, before the railways reached everywhere, horses were walked to race-meetings, and the route and the time it took applied the last fine touches to their preparation. Mr Hall planned on two days, with a night at an isolated inn, and men sent ahead to prepare. When we arrived at the race-course it was dusk, so that no touts or stable spies could get a clear glimpse of our horses.

There were camp fires, caravans and swarms of other grooms and stable lads. The grandstand was a black bulk and light flickered sometimes on posts and rails. A line of wooden stalls stretched away and Mr Hall's advance lads had taken the far end and put up a tent. We had a packhorse to carry feed and gear as well as the racers, and for supper were given half a loaf each and chops, which we skewered and cooked over a brazier. Mr Hall had a jar of pickled eggs in his saddlebag, and there was a fuss because someone had forgotten the salt.

We ate in Cloudy Mary's stall. She was quiet and happy with friends around her. When she lay down we slept in a huddle, some with her flank as a pillow – me, Jem, the stableboy, the jockey Jimmy Muggles and Trafalgar.

No-one except ourselves expected her to win with a boy up, and Mr Hall had spread gossip about Perambulator, his runner in the first race. He was in the form of his life and could not lose, everyone was told. Then of course he did lose, just as Mr Hall had planned.

At this, word spread among the hustlers, the know-alls, the connections of other horses, the bookmakers and the smart people in the grandstand or the carriages drawn up along the rails. Old Hall's messed it up this time, they said. He's miscalculated. For sure and for good and proper. His horses aren't in form at all. They're all over the place.

Then Cloudy Mary was saddled up and she leaned down to nuzzle Trafalgar. They breathed into each other's noses, as if to say "Be a sensible dog while I'm away!" and "I'm always sensible, which is why I know you can do it!"

The boy led her out. Mr Hall pretended to be gloomy and Jimmy Muggles to be nervous. I was entranced by the crowd: all sorts of folk and all sorts of entertainers, fire-eaters, rope-walkers, acrobats and fortune tellers. Our stable-lads said "Come on!" and we ducked under the rails, crossed the track, and scurried our way through the poorer people on the side opposite the grandstand. We ended up very near the winning post.

The start was out of our sight but we heard the shouts that began at the off and rolled nearer like a wave. Then around the curve came the blur of horses and men, but where were Jimmy's blue silks?

Cloudy Mary was small and at first look seemed always to struggle, but look again and see how her hooves hardly touched the turf, how she floated, how as unexpected as the weather she would quicken as the others laboured. So it was here.

She was behind. She could not find a way out. Jimmy's colours were hidden. Then there they were in the gap, and Jimmy seemed to do nothing, not to use his whip but to sit still and urge her with the calm shape of his body, and Cloudy Mary was ahead of them all and went past in a blur of blue and flying divots, and people yelled and cursed or were uplifted, and we knew that the money was landed, and went back to tell Trafalgar.

That victory was an exciting as anything I have seen, I

think, even Mr Macready in his famous death scene, which he acts with his back to the audience. In the happiness Jem confessed that he had plunged what was left of our money, and we had won enough to live on for several months. I was miffed that he had not warned me, but waited some days to tell him so, because I was sure that it was proof of our luck.

Cloudy Mary returned modest but proud, and lowered her head to Trafalgar, who licked it. There was glee and chatter that stopped in an instant and became awkward silence. A stranger stood there, tall and arrogant in a big and beautiful loose coat. He had servants with him, and handed his hat to one of them. Then he inspected Cloudy Mary through an eye-glass and said "No damage, Hall, I presume?"

"No damage, your Grace."

"Can we take her now?"

Mr Hall looked sad, but nodded.

"Markenfield won't lower the price, will he?"

"I'm instructed not, your Grace," said Mr Hall.

Cloudy Mary bridled and stamped, which was unusual, and men hushed and calmed her.

"Duke of Beverley," someone muttered in my ear.

"He's bought Cloudy Mary?" I said. "How could they sell?"

"Horseflesh," said the voice. "Markenfield's in debt."

Beverley said "Is this the dog that's supposed to keep her calm?"

"It is."

"What's his name?"

"Trafalgar," said Mr Hall, too uneasy to look at me.

"He's included in the price?"

"No, sir."

Beverley's long face seemed longer, but he exchanged a smile with one of his men.

"In that case," he said, "how much is he?"

Mr Hall did not want to answer.

"He's not for sale," I said.

Everybody looked.

"Who are you?" said Beverley.

"Polly Hindle, sir."

He scrutinised me through the eyeglass. I was annoyed because my dress was crushed and grubby.

"The dog's yours?"

"Yes, sir."

He confirmed it with a glance at Mr Hall and said "How much would she want for him?"

But before either of us could answer he pointed a finger.

"With that horse, this jockey and that dog we can win the Oaks and come back North for the Leger. How's that for a walk on the tightrope?"

"This jockey?" said Mr Hall

"Time for him to step up, Hall. You must see that. You've trained him to perfection."

"You'd take him down South?"

"No, no. Keep him here. Under wraps. Astonish the lot of them. What?"

Then the Duke turned to me and said "Twenty guineas?"

People gasped and Mr Hall stared as though to say that I was defiant at my own risk. I tried not to tremble.

"Sorry, sir," I said. "He's not for sale."

"Need him at home do you?"

"Don't have a home, sir. On the road, sir," said Jem.

Beverley peered at him.

"He's my brother, sir. It's the three of us."

"You and this ruffian and Trafalgar?"

"Yes, sir."

"What I'd do, sir," said Jem, "is take this old blanket with her."

Beverley's men wanted to cuff him, but the Duke himself held up a hand.

"There was a dog before Trafalgar." said Jem, "and if you ask me she'll take to another."

"Is this true?"

Mr Hall and various stableboys confirmed it.

"You mean the blanket smells of the whole sorry lot of you, so that she'll know you're still with her?"

"Yes, sir," said Jem. Then he realised his temerity and said "Sorry, sir. I'm very sorry, sir."

"No, no. Smart lad. Probably won't but could go far. Deal done!"

People sighed aloud. The Duke had been gracious, they acknowledged, and this pleased him. He twinkled his eyes at me, nodded at Mr Hall and went. His men led Cloudy Mary away there and then. Trafalgar growled but I held him.

"Markenfield's desperate for money, then," muttered someone.

"So he can keep gambling," said another.

"None of that!" said Mr Hall.

How could they take the horse that way, I thought. How could we have let them? Should I have let Trafalgar go, to stop Cloudy Mary being afraid? Would he have gone, actually, or would he have tried to run back to us? What do any of us mean to people who have money?

"That man," said Mr Hall "is His Majesty's Secretary of State for Foreign Affairs, and all you are is some snivelling girl."

But he grinned as he handed me Mr Swallow's letter to Mrs Whatshername.

We did not know it, but Jem and me were to meet the Duke of Beverley and Jimmy Muggles again, but not Mr Hall, because a few months later he died of the wheezing and spluttering that always made his discourse so comical.

CHAPTER TWENTY-ONE

As we walked into the city we did feel small and lonely and Jem said "What if nobody helps us?"

"We'll go to London," I replied.

"London?"

"London."

"Why?"

"It's where all the theatres are."

"Right-o!" said Jem. He nodded, muttered to himself, and walked with more purpose. Then he said "Does it matter that we look a mess?"

"A mess?"

He indicated my dress and his trousers. Both were grass-stained and muddy.

"Oh, come on, then!" I said, and we opened our bundles there and then and put on cleaner things, at the side of the road as people and carriages passed and someone shouted "Have you no shame?" I thought no, having been on the stage I don't. I'm used to being stared at.

We passed a horse-trough in which we splash-washed, and used as a mirror to comb our hair. So we felt spruce as we entered narrow old streets that were crooked and cobbled, and the upper stories leaned over us, and some shops had open fronts and wooden shutters. There were lots of people and we asked a woman selling ribbons for Scythegate, where the bookseller was. She pointed, we turned a corner and Jem said "I think that's it!"

A round-shouldered man in a skull-cup and apron watched a youth carry inside the second-hand volumes arrayed on a rickety table. There were maps in the window. We stared. The man opened his watch, consulted it, and looked up and down the street and at what sky could be seen between the gables. Then he noticed us.

"Please, sir," I said " we're from Mr Swallow."

The man clicked the watch shut, let it hang on its chain for a moment, and returned it to his waistcoat pocket. He made a sign to the youth, who hurried inside.

I wanted to speak but the man stopped me. People passed. We waited. A woman came out of the shop.

She was old and impatient. She looked at me and then questioned the bookseller with a jerk of her chin. You mean it's these two? He nodded.

"So what does he want?" she demanded. "Money, I suppose?"

Before I could reply she waved with contempt.

"Who are you anyway? Be off with you!"

She turned back and I shouted "Mr Swallow's dead."

In the silence this produced Jem said "Beg pardon. But are you the Queen of Yorkshire?"

She threw her stick at him. He fended it off and the shop boy snatched it from the cobbles. I tried to tell everything but the boy lashed at us. Trafalgar jumped and knocked the boy back, and we ran away.

I had been hit across the top of my arm and tried not to cry. What had we done wrong? Should we go back? Why had Mr Swallow said go to the bookshop first?

Then Jem said "Left. Right. Straight on. Left. Right."

"What?"

It was the way to the theatre. And anyway, said Jem, Mr Swallow never said speak to the bookseller. Yes he did. No he didn't. Hadn't he? I couldn't remember. Did he think that through us he would be forgiven for something? Don't be stupid, said Jem. I shoved him and it was at odds with each other that we came to the theatre, a new brick building when most of the city was of stone, and at least we knew that the place to go was the stage door.

When we were a few yards away the door flew open and a lad came out yelling "And you! And you!" and when he saw me he added "And you're not much, either! You're not much at all!" and with a rude gesture at Jem he was gone.

We had been told that the old city, once mighty, was now a drowsy sort of place, but all we had seen so far was angry people. We drew deep breaths, hoped for the best, and went inside.

Behind a half door with a counter top a plump little man with amazed eyebrows sat on a stool. Before I could stop him, Trafalgar put his front paws on the counter and almost licked the man's spectacles off his nose.

"Ah, well. Yes. Good evening, Canine Gentleman," said the man, and to me "What's his name, madam?"

"Trafalgar."

"Trafalgar. And Madam and Second Gentleman?"

Trafalgar flopped down and looked at me. He means you two, said his eyes.

"Polly Hindle," I said. "With my brother Jem."

"Never heard of any of you. Did you come in by mistake? What d'you want?"

I produced my letter.

"You're nowt to do with that fool who just left, are you?"

"Nothing. I've brought this letter for Mrs Whatshername."

He took it and said "As you see, it can wait in her pigeon hole."

"I can't do that," I said.

"You what?"

"It's personal," I said.

"You've to go back with a reply?"

I had not thought of that, and was flummoxed.

"Who's it from?" said the little man.

"Mr Swallow."

This checked him.

"Not strolling Swallow? Where is he?"

We told him.

"Oh," he said , "Oh, Lord."

For a moment I thought that he would cry but he collected himself and said "You'd better wait on that bench. Did you act with him?"

"Polly did," said Jem. "I'm like you."

"Really? By heck. What's that?"

"Unsung heroes," said Jem "who make it happen."

The man's spectacles were held together by black thread, I realised.

"It's Mr Fazackerley to you my lad," he said, "and we'll see about heroism as time passes."

Time did pass. We sat on the bench and Mr Fazackerley read a news sheet. Then Jem said "What's that noise?"

Mr Fazackerley looked at me and said "Can you hear it?"

"Yes," I said, although there was no definable sound at all. "What is it?"

"Ghosts."

"Ghosts?"

"The ghosts," said Mr Fazackerley "of all the words and energy that have been expended in this building."

Which it was, in that and every other theatre I have known, and while we listened to it people began to come in, collect keys, crack jokes, stare at us and go to their dressing rooms. Then Mr Fazackerley said "Canine Gentleman won't piss everywhere, will he?"

He would not, we assured him, and it was after one such mission, when I walked Trafalgar down the alley to look at the river and the quays and wherries and taverns there, that I returned to the stage-door and found Mr Fazackerley alone.

"Where's Jem?"
He pointed.
"Upstairs?"
"She came in," he said. "Mrs Whatshername."
"So Jem's with her?"
"Working."
"What?"
"Well, having sacked that fool you saw earlier we need a new call boy don't we? Now leave that dog here and go up yourself."

CHAPTER TWENTY-TWO

Mrs Whatshername had the most perfect blue eyes you ever saw, and had her chin been a fraction smaller she would have been an exceptional beauty. As it was, at that time in her life there was a weary dignity about her, a sweetness, a kindness and yet a sharpness of intent that made everyone respect her; as I did, from the moment she motioned me to sit on the couch, took my envelope, and opened it. There was a covering note from Mr Eaton, which she read first, and the page that Mr Swallow had dictated and managed to sign.

When Mrs Whatshername read this she smiled back a tear, and for an instant seemed unsure of what to do. The dressing room was full of her costumes, creams, wigs and potions. A fire crackled. There were more candles than Mr Swallow's theatre could ever have afforded. As though she read this comparison she asked me what had happened and how he died, and out of nothing said "So what happened to Beaumont?"

"Beaumont?"

"The horse?"

"I didn't know him. I knew Fletcher."

"Fletcher," she said. "Of course. Fletcher. Then she laughed, and said "But what about – ?"

But a man came in, and because he had not knocked I knew that it was Mr Whatshisname. He was smaller than I had expected, but with a big head, and a crude handsomeness. He glanced at me, and then at her without interest, and said "Is this the girl?"

She passed him the letter and smiled at me to say "Don't worry."

He read, and when he looked up it was with a different expression, not personal but logical and neutral, as if to measure or count. He saw not just my body without clothes, but the bones inside my flesh. Then he smiled the smile that I knew later to be suited to the characters he played, the Richard the Thirds, the Iagos, the Emperors and the calculating adventurers, and then he was himself again.

"Well proportioned," he said. "Excellent eyes. See them from the back of the hall. Doesn't flinch when stared at. Movement?"

I curtseyed low and rose high again.

"Like you," he said to his wife, "Smart old Swallow. What about her voice?"

"The poor world is almost six thousand years old," I said, as if to an audience in a field, "and in all this time there was not any man died in his own person, videlicet, in a love cause. Troilus had his brains dashed out with a Grecian club, yet he did what he could do to die before, and he is one of the patterns of love."

"Old plays," he said. "Who taught you that?"

"I read it."

"And remembered it at once?"

Yes, I had. From one of Mr Eaton's Shakespeare volumes.

Mrs Whatshername watched him with an air of triumph that he resented, I thought, but could not deny. She took the letters from his fingers and in a dreamy way put them to the flame of a candle, so that they flared and then turned to petals of ash, which she let fall into her waste basket. So I will never read them now, I thought. Except that I did know, because Jem had overheard Mr Eaton explain in confidence to the horse trainer Mr Hall.

When you have met and heard her I am sure that you will

agree, my dearest daughter Whatsyourname, that however long we live this is the best actress we will see. And for my sins, to your schooling I entrust her.

CHAPTER TWENTY-THREE

Schooling is the word for what happened in the next years of our lives, and it began at once, when we were introduced to a Mr Joseph Acklam and sent in his care to watch that evening's performance.

What a joy and shock to see a proper theatre! We were in a jewel box, with the stage and its apron, the Pit, the boxes full of gentry, the smoke and magic of candles everywhere, the tops of so many heads as we leaned over the Gallery.

Mr Acklam sat between us. His clothes were new and clean, and of good cloth, but seemed too old for him, because he was a youth, eager one moment and shy the next. He giggled at himself but frowned at the loud, smelly, pushing, coarse-spoken, jolly mob around us. When we asked a question he said "You'll need to ask me that later," and offered us another striped humbug. Altogether he was a bad case of what I call the muttery-fidgets, and the reason was that he was the co-author with Mr Whatshisname of the play we were about to see.

Entitled 'The Handicapped Suitor' it was a novelty knocked up for race week, and told a story of true love lost and found among a party of local gentry up for the races. There were comic servants and a rascally horse-doper, and I confess that despite his jitters I gazed at Mr Acklam with some awe, because he was the first real writer we had met.

"Would Shakespeare have had a bag of humbugs?" asked Jem later, and I said "No, because he was acting the Ghost." Mr Acklam, quipped Jem, was more like the person haunted.

As the play unfolded, and Mr Whatshisname as the

impoverished suitor disguised himself as a girl, and Mrs Whatshername the unattainable object of his desire disguised herself as a boy, Mr Acklam winced, slumped with his face in his hands, and once or twice cried out "Yes!"

When I understood things better, which was after not many months, I did wonder if Mr Acklam had been sent to the Gallery less to protect Jem and me than in the hope that he would learn from the spectators. It was obvious what they liked, disliked and found comical, and their applause was warm enough. But Mr Acklam had little time for them. He either spluttered with pleasure at this own cleverness, or snarled about brutes and illiterate savages.

"It must be fairyland, though," said Jem later, "to write your own play and see it acted," and indeed I have supposed ever since that it must, because for us it was fairyland to sit there.

After the play there was a novelty item in which two men danced blindfold between a dozen eggs without breaking them, and then the one act Afterpiece, and a specially written Epilogue to conclude. This drew a few morals, thanked the town for its patronage and described what would be played the next night.

It was while the stage manager was restoring the unbroken eggs to their basket that I dared to ask a question.

"Have you written other plays, Mr Acklam?"

"What? Oh. Yes. Seven."

"Seven."

"Two are partly in Latin," he said. "Don't raise your voices. We don't want these barbarians to know who I am."

"Where were they performed?" persisted Jem.

"They weren't."

"Never? Not ever? Why not?"

"Because as even you must realise from these oafs around us," said Mr Acklam, "the public taste is neither informed nor elevated."

We wanted him to explain this but a huge clap of stage thunder introduced the Afterpiece. It was a melodrama about a murderer trapped in a haunted house, which transpired to be his own nightmares. For at least the next two years Mr Whatshisname and Mr Acklam tried to work this up into a five-acter, but never did so because although the beginning was chilling and they had the end, they never agreed upon what should happen in the middle.

CHAPTER TWENTY-FOUR

Discussions about plays, how they had once been, how they were now, and how they might be again, and about how our audience was different from that in London, and what they each wanted and why, were as long and interesting as any I had with Mrs Whatshername, if not as long as those about clothes.

How to alter and care for clothes and make them last: how to look appropriate: how to appraise myself and trim a fashion to my own size and shape and colouring. How not to look a mess , darling, that's the thing. Although in truth, she would say, we're both pretty perfect clothes horses.

And other things. How to detect when an actor would be a good or bad influence within a company. How to spot a ticket seller on the fiddle. How to please tradespeople, so that they would spread the word, support a Benefit Performance, and not demand their money too soon. How to treat a journalist with care. What to pack when the company was on tour. How to look fresh on arrival. How to concentrate, and not waste energy.

She would make little comments about people, but she did not gossip as such. I'm the leading lady, darling. I can't gossip. I'm gossiped about.

How to maintain that status. What to do when theatre managers try to get you to do more than you were contracted for, such as adding dates and venues, and printing bills that announce the leading tragedians in the Afterpiece as well as the play. How, when you are the manager yourself, to wangle the opposite.

And how not to parade deep feelings, to keep in the past what lay in the past, so that someone such as me could deduce without being told that I should never ask about Mr Swallow, the bookseller and the Queen of Yorkshire. I would know about them or not, as need dictated.

Childhood is discovery, she said, and we are grown up when we accept our ignorance.

These opinions were given straight, as from a Mother to a daughter. What she taught me about acting itself was off-hand, almost. She encouraged me to do what felt right, even if it was a mistake, and then made me think about it when I least expected to do so, as on the morning we returned from the fishmongers and happened to see the departure of the Mail Coach.

"Look at these two," said Mrs Whatshername. "What do you think?"

A young man said goodbye to an older woman, walked to the coach, and before he swung up to the roof looked back.

"He's leaving her," I said. "She won't see him again."

"How do you know that?"

How did I know? Was it the woman? No. Her back was to us.

"The way he looked back," I said. "He didn't turn his body."

"Suppose he had?"

"He'd have been sorry to leave," I said, "but now he isn't."

The Guard blew his horn and off the coach clattered. Mrs Whatshername changed the subject, but that night she played a farewell scene with her husband. He was at the front corner of the stage and she at the far back, and when she angled her body towards him the pause and the space between them so ached with emotion that someone in the Gallery yelled "She will return! She will!" and people gasped. When she came off she passed me and said "The Royal Mail, darling, remember?"

CHAPTER TWENTY-FIVE

Jem had been made a call boy at once, and soon assisted in all departments, including the way he pestered Mr Whatshisname to explain why he charged different prices in different parts of the theatre, and at different times of the year, and how the cost of playbills and flyers varied according to the number printed, and on what sort of paper. Trafalgar became very at home in Mr Fazackerley's cubby-hole and indeed sometimes guarded it himself, but for months I was confined to small parts, or the crowd, or even nothing at all except Mrs Whatshername's dresser.

Jem and me and Trafalgar shared an attic in a house where two or three other actors lodged, but sometimes I slept on a truckle bed at the foot of Mrs Whatshername's four-poster. Mr Whatshisname had his own room. He was rarely in hers, although sometimes during the day they would lock themselves in her dressing room and I would sit on the stone stairs outside, and move further down so as not to hear their voices and her cries.

This is an apt memory at which to say that I learned more in those years than how to live in a properly run, if provincial theatre. I experienced above all the changes in my body that transformed me from a girl into a woman, and in consequence I received the attentions of men.

This flustered me. I had never felt what many girls feel – depression because they are plain or imagine themselves to be so. Mother had looked good and so do I, I thought, and after all I was soon on stage and people stared. No, what disconcerted me was my desire to respond to looks and touches and blatant suggestions. I knew that I could take someone to my breast as a woman. I could have a child.

What would that be like? Should I try to find out? Would I have the opportunity? Would men always want me in that way? What if something else about me bored them or put them off? If there was something about me that people disliked, what would it be? Then one night I was on stage and I thought maybe I speak my mind when I shouldn't or maybe I talk about Trafalgar all the time, or maybe –

Actors were staring at me. I had missed my cue.

"Where were you?" said Jem afterward, "what happened?"

"Mind you own business," I snapped.

Then I thought: this is ridiculous. I'm me. And I know that there is someone in the world who will respect that, and be thrilled by it. The only question is: will I meet him?

After this it became part of life, as it is for all women. And to a degree for all men, I suppose, because they can lord it and be conceited and belittle us for ever, but what they need most is our approval. When we know this it is for us not to take advantage of them, although this can be difficult; and if men who are violent in private are what women dread, those who mope in public are the most annoying. Mr Acklam was one of them.

He did not lean over me, or make remarks, or try to catch me bending over backstage, or appear on staircases to reveal certain parts of his anatomy. No. All Mr Acklam did was stare.

Everybody noticed it but what could be done? Jem said "Shall I kick his shin?" Mr Fazackerley said "Writing Gentleman's a complete wet what-not!" Mr Whatshisname was supposed to have had a word but no-one was sure that that he had, even when Mr Acklam did not appear for weeks on end.

I did not ask the reason because I did not want to draw

attention, or make people think that I might be interested. Even as it was, the younger actresses made it a joke at my expense.

"If Mr Acklam stared at you, Emily, what would you do?"

"I'd put a stop to it, Abigail, that's what I'd do. What would you do Polly?"

In truth I did not know what to do. I felt foolish again, and other people seemed to think me so. Mr Acklam was older than me, and educated, which I was not; and although I had always thought him comical I did not want to upset him. But why, when he re-appeared, did he continue to moon about? Why was he afraid to speak to me, let alone touch me? At the very least, I thought, he should give me the chance to refuse.

Sometimes I found scraps of paper between the pages of my playscript, on which he had written verses such as

> I worship but cannot see
> Because of tears between you and me

But how was I supposed to respond? How, indeed, was I supposed to know who the versifier was?

That was the annoyance, I decided. I can confess now that at this time I had a passion of my own, for a coal-heaver on the wharf. But he had a wife and children and mates and why would he care about a thin girl like me? We spoke on Trafalgar's walks but my demeanour revealed nothing, and one day I saw him drunk and vomiting and thought: no.

But I had respected him. Mr Acklam did not respect me, and did not trust me, because if he had he would have made an open declaration, verbal or physical. That he did not do so meant that he cared more about his own feelings than mine. So much for silent worship then! So much for being blinded by tears!

Ludicrous, I thought, and the next time he sat at the side of the stage and stared at me during rehearsals I waited until my second scene was finished, walked up to him and said "Mr Acklam, I'm very sorry, but if you're helpless with love for me why don't you ask me to marry you?" He looked aghast. He stared wild-eyed. Then he smirked and said "Very well. Polly Hindle, will you do me the honour of becoming my wife?"

"No," I said. "Certainly not. Why?"

"Do you want me to ask the Whatshisnames," he said, "in loco parentis?"

"In what?"

"It's Latin. It means, in place of your parents?"

"No," I said. "I'm me – I'm myself."

"But how old are you?"

"What's that got to do with it?"

"I don't think you know your own mind."

Men say that, don't they? Even when we blush at ourselves later, they say that we don't know our own minds.

"Of course I know my own mind."

"Oh. Do you? Well. Do you know what my Mother says?"

"I don't care what your Mother says."

"She says that all actresses are loose women and have been for centuries, but nobody—"

"What?"

"Nobody listens to me, do they, when I—"

"Loose women?"

"When I say please God why can't my Mother drop dead and leave me the money and—"

He realised that everyone had stopped work to stare at us, even Jem at the top of the ladder.

"Act Two Scene Two, Polly. Your entrance with the poisonous snake. When you're ready," said Mr Whatshisname.

"Sorry," I said, and walked toward him with my line of dialogue.

"Oh woe is me, for what is this I've done?"

What indeed, muttered a voice inside me, but later Mrs Whatshername and I took a turn together in the alley. "Good girl," she said, and everyone else seemed to think so as well, but when I saw how Mr Acklam skulked I felt mean. He was more hang-dog than Trafalgar when he is chastised for shaking mud and water everywhere. I touched his sleeve and said "Mr Acklam, be assured. I have no wish to wound you, or jeopardise our friendship."

"Thank you," he said, "I knew you'd understand."

"Really!" I said to Jem later. "Really! As soon as his feelings were mentioned he was happy!"

"Maybe you should have declared yourself to the coal-heaver," said Jem, with a mock gloomy expression, and I boxed his ears, for what come to think of it was the last time ever.

In bed I thought: how did he know about the coal-heaver? What else has he seen? Is he sharper than me? Am I hopeless? Am I the romantic? Airy fairy? Then snappy when it suits me? Why do girls doubt themselves all the time, and boys never? I was in charge until this absurd Mr Acklam business and now look at me. When, oh when will I grow up?

CHAPTER TWENTY-SIX

Is it surprising that what happened next was that Mr Acklam became my best friend after Jem? Not really. As I began to be cast in bigger roles, to act from experience as well as instinct and to be liked by the audience, the other supporting actresses grew suspicious. They were civil, and we twittered away in the dressing room, but I was on my guard. This was not least the case because the theatre's business declined.

The city was surrounded by hundreds and thousands of acres of farm-land, and agricultural prices were falling. There was less money to spend, and hardship, and people were less sure of who they were and what they wanted.

Mr Fazackerley, who had kept the stage door for three previous managers, and been a call-boy for Mr Whatshisname's Father, said "Option Gentleman, Madam Polly, Option Gentleman." By which he meant that Mr Whatshisname was considering his options, and it was rumoured that one of them would be to reduce the number of players, which is why the actresses could be niggly.

"But if they go it isn't your fault," said Mr Acklam, "and in any case my situation is far more desperate."

I was used to this. He was trapped, he said, between the call of his inspiration and this duty to his Mother. He would never be able to do what he wanted.

"What is that?"

He could never explain.

"And as for going to Newcastle," he said, "how can I leave Mother to do that?"

Newcastle? It was the latest rumour, he said, and an old theme among provincial managers. When they and the public exhausted each other managers moved on, and took a theatre in another town.

"Is this true?" I asked Jem. "What have you heard?"

He promised to sniff around. If it was true we should move ourselves, we knew, and so should Mr Acklam. If I am truly his friend, I thought, I must give him a shake.

"Set out on your own," I said. "Just go, You can always run back to your Mother."

"Set out? I need a theme!"

"Ancient Egypt," I said, out of nothing.

"Egypt?"

"Isn't that a grand theme for you?"

"Why can't women understand?" he said.

Which were the last words he spoke to me, because he went home and never returned. Enquiries two days later revealed he had taken a commercial stagecoach, and nobody heard any more about him. Until now, that is, when he is famous as the writer of lurid books about Ancient Egypt, Babylon, and the Holy Land.

So whatever might have happened had I married Mr Acklam, I think it is fair to say that I influenced him. What happened to his Mother I do not know, and even Jem has been unable to discover.

CHAPTER TWENTY-SEVEN

Rumours about Mr Whatshisname's intentions continued to infest the backstage and the taverns around the theatre. He had saved enough money to retire, said one, and another concerned me.

"Miss Juliet can't play Juliet all her life, can she Gentleman Jem?" said Mr Fazackerley, and what he meant was that Mrs Whatshername would soon be too old to play young lovers and heroines in distress. "What's your opinion, Gentleman Jem?" probed Mr Fazackerley, "has Madam Polly been brought in to replace her?"

For all my ambition I hoped that this was not the case, and I discussed with Jem what to do if it was proposed. We had all heard stories of unhappiness when manager husbands replaced actress wives, and I did not want to be a part of it. I admired Mrs Whatshername. She was my friend and still had more to teach me. But if the issue was forced we would leave, we decided.

Then Mr Whatshisname surprised everyone by hiring as an attraction in our forthcoming race-week season the London favourite Mr Rathbone.

When the London theatre season ended in the late spring its leading performers sought to rake in money by touring the country as guest artists, and we had entertained our fair share. But they were invariably tragedians. Mr Rathbone was not. He was a comedian, and hiring him was a smart move and made money.

He was a stately little person who walked with exaggerated care, and what had made his name was his ability to play both high and low comedy. He could be an indignant Father or deceived husband one minute, and a vulgar face-pulling farting knockabout the next. This meant that he could appear in the main bill one night and the Afterpiece the next, and for more money or a Benefit Night he would appear in both.

As was the custom, we rehearsed the plays without him so that he could perform upon arrival. This did mean that he could be acting one thing and we another, but he overcame these problems by ruthless upstaging and attention-grabbing antics.

Offstage Mr Rathbone brought all the news and tittle-tattle from London and elsewhere. He came to us from playing two nights with a company in Birmingham, which he described as a dog's breakfast. Since Trafalgar has always been a very tidy eater I am in two minds about that expression, and heaven knows how Mr Rathbone described us; but I did take the opportunity of a quiet moment to say "Beg pardon, Mr Rathbone, but have you ever heard in London of an actor called Tom Dorchester?"

"Never. Who is he? Never."

In any case, the latest London sensations, and the ones the Whatstheirnames wanted to ask about, and Mr Rathbone to tell, were Miss Faucit, an actress of my age engaged to play opposite the mighty Mr Macready, and a young man named Wareham.

"What's he made of?" said Mr Whatshisname.

"Haven't seen him. Outer London. A lot of shouting, I daresay. But she's marvellous."

"Outer London?" muttered Jem.

"Theatres half a mile from the West End, love," said someone. "Enormous. Can't see a little actor, never mind hear him."

"As I say," continued Mr Rathbone, "Macready's all gloom

and Faucit's all light. Clever contrast. Very emotional. One night she fainted on stage. Taken to her room. Talk of the town. Now. Where can I buy an oyster?"

At the end of the week he left us. Two months later, when we were rehearsing topical Afterpieces for the week of the Assizes, Mr Fazackerley stopped me at the stage-door and said "Thunder and lightning, Madam Polly, but there's a letter for you."

"A what?"

"From London."

"I don't know anyone in London."

He handed me the letter, thick creamy paper, folded and sealed with red wax, and the London Office mark stamped as clear as day. I was so eager that I made a small tear in the paper.

"Slit the wax," said Mr Fazackerley, as he handed me a penknife. "Did no-one ever write to you before?"

I slit the wax and returned the penknife and wanted to open the sheet out. But I thought the better of it and said "Thank you" and went to my dressing-room.

It's from Father, I thought. He's safe and he wants us and – Then I realised that I did not know the handwriting, nor, when I glanced at the bottom of the opened page, the signatory. Yours in anticipation, Thaddeus Stephen. Thaddeus Stephen? I had never heard of him. Then I read what he had written.

My dear Miss Hindle – on the recommendation of Mr Samuel Rathbone, who described your performances in detail, and at the behest of Mr Edward Wareham, of whose company at the Fitzroy Theatre I am the manager, I write to offer you a twelve weeks engagement at—

CHAPTER TWENTY-EIGHT

Jem read the letter twice, with great care. The second paragraph said that since Mr Rathbone had been advised that I was unlikely to travel without my brother Mr Jem Hindle, they would offer him a position backstage, and that if we notified them of our acceptance of the indicated terms they would advance the money for us to travel to London by the Heavy Stage Coach. Jem snorted and refolded the letter.

"No mention of Trafalgar," he said.

"But what d'you think?"

"You're not scared are you?"

"Of course I'm scared."

I was. Scared of London, and scared of having to speak to Mr and Mrs Whatshisname.

"If I said no I wouldn't need to tell them, would I?"

"How d'you know he's not written to them as well?"

I recalled Mr Fazackerley's foxy alertness. Of course there had been another letter.

"A bit earlier than we planned," said Jem, "but I reckon you're ready."

"I'll talk to Mrs Whatshername right now."

She was in her dressing room and sewing, because she took care herself of all her stage clothes. I opened my mouth but was not sure what to say. She smiled and said "Have they written to you as well, then?"

"Yes."

"And do you want to go?"

"Do you think I'm good enough?" I said.

"Don't you?"

"I'm not sure."

"Don't you want to find out?"

"Were you good enough?" I blurted, and winced at my own impertinence.

"I married Mr Whatshisname," she said.

Of course she was good enough, I thought. She must have been extraordinary. Then life dimmed her. I realised that in this one conversation I could ask her anything, and that she would answer.

"You never had children," I said.

"Miscarried."

"Oh."

"Then I couldn't," she said. "Or maybe wouldn't. Gentleman can wear armour, you know."

I blushed. I did know. They put silk or muslin protectors over that certain part of their anatomy. The other actresses giggled about it.

"In London, Miss Polly, you'll need to be aware of that. Many theatre girls are no better than they should be. You must tread a fine line."

"Who's the old lady at the booksellers?" I interrupted.

She hesitated. But what had she to lose, now?

"She's my Mother."

"But you don't visit her?"

"No."

"I miss my Mother every day," I said.

"I suppose I ran off with my Father."

"Mr Swallow?"

"Yes."

"Why did you come back?"

But I know why. She married, and they took the theatre.

"And who is the Queen of Yorkshire?" I said.

She sighed. She wore a dress whose colours had faded, and

so had her eyes and hair. I felt the power of my youth, and her fear of it.

"Would Mr Whatshisname release me?" I said.

"Yes," she smiled, "if I say that he should. Of course he'll release you."

CHAPTER TWENTY-NINE

What a journey it was! What a wearisome, uncomfortable thrill, that when I think of it now is a jumble of jolted-awake moments! Since Mr Wareham's people would not pay for us to take the Mail we booked the overnight Heavy Stage called the 'Express', which was a misnomer. 'Express' kept more or less to the Mail's ten miles an hour, but stopped at many more places, and took many more short-stage passengers, so that there was more confusion, and more worry that our bundles would be chucked out with other peoples'. And there was Trafalgar. When we booked Jem at three pence a mile outside and me at five pence a mile inside, Trafalgar was refused. At the Driver's discretion, they said, so when 'Express' came in Jem over-tipped both the Driver and the Guard and Trafalgar either sprawled on the roof or ran in the road with the horses. It was after four when we left, with the coach-lamps lit, and Mrs Whatshername very straight backed as she watched us go.

I had tried to secure a seat with my back to the horses, but I was shoved aside by a bossy man and had to crush in, next to a very fat woman. There was straw around our feet and the coach was old and smelly, and unpleasant when the window was closed. When it was not the draught made my eyes sting.

At first my inside companions chattered and compared stories, although I kept as silent as I could because I was not sure that they would approve of an actress. Then they tired and dozed and in the darkness lanterns bobbed as other conveyances rushed past, distant furnaces glared and at one town halt Jem stamped his feet, stamp, stamp, stamp because they were so cold he could not feel them.

Inns prided themselves on smooth exchanges, four horses walked out of the traces and four backed in, the driver up again, new passengers pleased with themselves, old ones dazed and aching all over, people shouting, urchins running, and the Guard bugling.

Then half sleep again, then in dawn mist a forest, then pitched awake again as 'Express' halted and wooden blocks were shoved under the rear wheels. Down clambered the driver in his caped topcoat, and a skivvy bought him a mug of ale. I rushed to the inn privy, and almost before I had time to wipe myself heard the summons of the bugle. Jem had bought poke-fulls of sliced beef and hot potato, and I scrambled back.

I was awoken from another bad sleep by clamour and rush all around. "It's London! It's London!" But it was not. It was the last stop at the Peacock Inn, Islington, and the next downhill miles were those into the city itself: into the stenches of its manure, human and animal, its smoke, its foul little industries, and the blood even, of the cattle market that was hard by Newgate Prison and our destination the Saracens Head Inn.

Through threadbare stinking crowds, old men wearing sandwich boards, shouting women who tried to sell bundles of tired watercress, an energy, an excitement, the challenge of a sense that although money was being grabbed from the air nobody had any, 'Express' trundled at walking pace to the huge inn yard. There the roar of the city was distant like the tide outside a breakwater and sounds were individual: hooves, harness, ostlers, baggage thumps and cries of farewell and greeting.

But who was there to greet us? No-one. We went into the Travellers Rooms and asked the cashier but he poo-poohed us and said that his business was to take money, not give advice. There were six or eight coaches outside, some arrived, some about to depart, and many people.

My head swam and I slumped on a bench. I closed my eyes. I did not even want to think. Then someone shouted from the doorway. It was an ostler, I saw.

"Trafalgar!" he yelled again "Name of Trafalgar!"

I heard Trafalgar himself in the yard but where was Jem? I stumbled out. Jem had a silly grin, and Trafalgar bounced up and down in front of Tom Dorchester, whose clothes were dandified.

"Well," he said, "Miss Polly Bowler, and not before time!"

"You?" I said. "Where's Mr Wareham? What's happening?"

"I'm Wareham," he grinned, "Dorchester. Wareham. What's in a name? Come on!"

I did, but found it hard, because from the sudden weak feeling in my knees, and some lurch in my stomach, I knew that I loved him, and not as a girl who has a crush for an older man, but as a woman, who knows that she is bound to this person, and open to him, for better or worse, and for what at the time seems forever.

CHAPTER THIRTY

I had discovered my passion but did not want to reveal it. I said little and tried to be demure. I would not betray to the world what should be obvious to Tom alone. Should he not perceive at once that I loved him, and be the one to take the initiative, to hold and kiss and reassure me, to uphold me with his strength which itself drew strength from what I felt for him? He should. But he did not.

He had a rickety one-horse cab to take us to the half-built square in Bloomsbury where he lodged in Admiral Wood's boarding house with other actors, a young lawyer's clerk and an engraver's colourist and his wife. Me and Jem would have an attic, he said, and Admiral Wood was not a real admiral but, according to his latest story, a former officer in the army of the East India Company. He had a wooden leg and lived on the raised ground floor.

"Wooden leg?" said Jem.

"Mauled by a tiger. Or so he says."

"You mean he tells lies?"

"He's a romancer," said Tom. "Aren't we all?"

Not a word about how he betrayed Mr Swallow and ran off to suit himself. And I didn't care. I was in love and didn't care.

"I've still got your guinea," I said.

"What?"

"The one you gave me when you jumped up on to the Mail."

"Did I?"

I must have looked hurt.

"Come on, Bowler! Grand adventure! Ophelia to Hamlet! Juliet to Romeo!"

There was caution in Jem's eyes. He understands, I realise. He's seen it, like he saw it with the coal-heaver.

"Is Mrs Whatshername effective?" Tom rattled on. "The husband's a face-puller, isn't he, but old Rathbone says that she could have been good."

Defend her, I thought. And then: it's not personal, it's about a craft. Before I could say something measured we went from noisy ugliness into the quiet of a half-completed square. There was still a market garden in the middle, and the roadway was half mud and half wooden blocks.

"Crikey!" said Jem. "Are these gas lamps?"

"Gas," said Tom, and then "Oh no! Oh my God! Drive round! Keep driving!"

"What?"

I looked out. A shouting man waved a cudgel, two women pulled at him and on a doorstep a distinguished-looking man pointed a pistol. One of his white trouser legs was hemmed up over a wooden leg.

"Stop!" I cried, and my tone was so sharp that the driver obeyed. Dog, bundles and passengers were flung together. Sunlight gleamed on Tom's hair. He grinned. He looked wonderful.

"Steady on, Bowler," he said, "you always knew that I enjoy the ladies."

"Outraged Father?" I said. "Weeping Mother? Girl who thinks you'll take her to Paris?"

"How d'you know that?" he said.

"It's the play!" realised Jem.

"What play?"

"It's called 'The Blackguard's Downfall'" I said. "Rewritten by Mr Swallow. And we all know what comes next!"

I scrambled out, and strode to the enraged group. The

Father recognised Tom and shouted "There's the black devil himself!"

He launched himself. Trafalgar snarled. The Father stopped. He looked from dog to people to pistol. I could remember my old dialogue and improvised where necessary.

"I am that Emily Huntingbridge of whom you have heard," I said, "and this is the Certificate of my marriage to Mr Wareham. Leave forthwith, and take your unfortunate daughter with you."

I have to admit that in a cheap and sullen sort of way the girl was beautiful, even as beautiful as me, I feared, and I did not have marriage lines or any piece of paper in my hand, but my acting must have had force because the Father hurled his cudgel at Tom, who caught it in his left hand. The Father yelled at the women to follow and stormed off.

Silence. Then Jem applauded and workmen in the garden joined in, and Tom said "That pistol isn't loaded, is it?"

"Certainly not," said Admiral Wood, and pulled the trigger. Flash. Bang. Powder stink. Splinters flew as the bullet whipped into a tree.

"Miss Bowler?" said the Admiral. "Privileged to meet you, ma'am. And Corporal Hindle, I presume?"

Jem looked round, saw no-one else, and said "I suppose I must be, sir."

"Play cards, do you?"

"I'm sure you can show me, Admiral," replied Jem, which was wicked of him, because Mr Hall's grooms and jockeys had taught him more trick shuffles than a monkey.

"House Rule Number One is feet," said the Admiral. "Wipe that magnificent dog's feet. As I've told Mr Wareham, I don't care what trollops he brings in but I won't have unscraped boots."

He waved us inside and Jem said: "His waistcoat's marvellous. I want one."

A wish that came true, because today he is known all over theatreland as the diminutive power-broker with the pomaded hair, the gold rings, the cigars and the rainbow waistcoats, which, I have more that once told him, Mother and Father would have found ostentatious. His reply is always the same, "It's a fairground, love, and all I am is a showman."

"Fairground? We're trying to do Shakespeare properly."

"So you gain from the contrast, don't you? A pure deed in a naughty world."

Which I suppose is true. My hair has for years been long again, and I often hold it in ribbons, and I learned from Mrs Whatshername the dignity of muted hues and simple lines. Polly Hindle is a simple person, whose hopes and memories are private. Polly Bowler is the attention-seeker, and most of her life is on stage.

CHAPTER THIRTY-ONE

There were people in every room of the Admiral's house, from the Indian cook in the back basement kitchen, the colourist and his wife at the front, Wood himself on most of the ground floor, Tom, the actors and the lawyer's clerk as we went up, a skivvy named Sukie in the front attic and me and Jem and Trafalgar in the back. Our window overlooked rooftops. There were two privies in the yard and we soon learned that water was a problem.

London was bursting and building, and water and street lights were slow to follow. There was no water in our square yet and Sukie and the cook would take buckets to a stand-pipe which was not always turned on. Most Londoners were unwashed and smelled and we theatricals were lucky to have scented powders as part of our trade.

That first night me and Jem had half a basinful to wash in and we would need to use it again in the morning. "And don't tip it then" we were told, "just in case." Our attic had a narrow bed, a chest, a chamber pot and a hammock, in which Jem swung very happily and let me use as a treat on birthdays.

"I must find a mirror," I said, and blew out the candle. Beyond our darkness the city still roared. Not until then did Jem speak.

"Ask me, I think you love him. Don't you?"

"What?"

"You heard," he said.

"What if I do?"

"He thinks you're a sort of tom-boy sister."

"He'll want me in the end," I said.

"What if he doesn't?"

"He will."

Silence.

"So you trust him?" he said.

"Yes."

"Despite what we know he's done?"

"There's something wonderful in him," I said, "and in the end he'll respect it."

No reply. I began to speak but stopped. Better to say nothing than be at odds, I thought. I was almost asleep when he spoke again.

"If Tom's the theatre management, where did he get the money?"

"Go to sleep," I said. But I knew that we had both made the same guess, I voiced it.

"If it was from a woman," I said, "it just depends on who, and how old she is."

"I'll find out," said Jem, and no more was said.

CHAPTER THIRTY-TWO

Next morning our London life began in earnest. We washed in the greasy water and saved it, which was just as well because we needed it that night and the following morning, and walked to the theatre through streets that were an amazement of dust, noise and street sellers. Tom was in one of those moods when nervousness made him excitable, and he rushed us from one part of the theatre to another.

It was bigger and fancier that anything we had seen. It had the latest gas footlights, an orchestra pit, a Green Room for the actors, and all sorts of scenic machinery. When we sat in one of the boxes I thought "My Lord, but will I make myself heard in this vastness?"

"Of course you will! Breathe in! Breathe out!" enthused Tom, and then glanced at me sideways like a little boy in trouble. "My oath, Bowler, but how did you know I told that girl I'd take her to Paris?"

"Did you mean to?"

"Never."

"So you were acting?"

"I was being a seducer, wasn't I?"

"That's all very well," I said, "so long as you know what's real and what's not."

"I don't," he said. "Not always."

"What?"

"Well" – he began, and described how a few days before he had been for a walk in a jungle which he had thought was a turning off Regent Street. He had been overwhelmed by the scent of huge flowers, and there were monkeys with bright green eyes. Then he laughed and said "But I always told you stories like that, didn't I?"

He did. He made miserable moorland nights in Mr Swallow's wagon seem magical, and we had dreamed our dreams.

"Can we do it, Tom?" I said now. "Can we ever be famous?"

"My oath but we can," he replied. "We can show them how to act. I sent for you, didn't I? It can happen to us!"

Which it did: much sooner, and in a more unexpected fashion, than we had imagined.

CHAPTER THIRTY-THREE

The bricks and mortar of Tom's Fitzroy Theatre were owned by its speculative builder, who had leased the use of them to an old dog of an actor manager named Thaddeus Stephen. Mr Stephen specialised in burlettas, plays which because they had music could pass as operas, and did not need a licence. He engaged Tom as a useful sort of fellow who could come up with a Prologue, rewrite an Afterpiece, carry a tune and play small parts, such as the first Tragedian's best friend.

"But when you look at me," Tom had complained, "don't you see a heroic actor?"

"No," Mr Stephen would say. "Get on with them rhyming couplets."

Covent Garden, Drury Lane and the Haymarket were the theatres in which reputations were made, and Tom left Mr Stephen and played small parts in all three. He attracted attention and moved in a lively crowd. One night he went after a performance to drink in the Argyle Divan, a cigar lounge off Piccadilly that was not as respectable as it might have been, and he heard the red-hot gossip: just an hour earlier Mr Stephen had been on stage in the part of a jovial uncle, which was how he saw himself even though he was a notorious penny-pincher, when he was struck by a seizure and carried speechless to his lodgings.

Next afternoon Tom made an offer to take over the lease of the theatre, and it was accepted for the sake of the widowed niece with whom Mr Stephen lived. Mr Stephen himself was supposed to die, but did not, and Tom invited him back as a sort of manager-cum-sphinx-to-be-consulted: a hulk with restricted movement and little coherent speech, but a brain still immaculate as clockwork.

All this had happened before we were sent for, and when we arrived Jem was put in with Mr Stephen. They were soon a wily combination, the cheeky apprentice and the ruined sorcerer, who communicated through grunts, head shakes, and messages scrawled left-handed because his right was frozen.

Tom wanted to change everything but the Fitzroy audience loved burlettas and would have to be respected. Also, there was very little money, and Tom did not own any plays. His solution was to steal one.

It was outrageous of course, but not unusual at the time, and seemed to be a lark when we watched over three nights the play he had chosen, and I memorised an act at a time and then spoke it back to Tom and Jem by candlelight, or the next morning. Then when we read the whole thing we did not like it.

Admiral Wood heard us regurgitate some of it and said it was namby-pamby. Mr Stephen thought it so bad that he moaned and rocked like a caged bear. We felt glum. Maybe we weren't as clever as we thought. Then Jem said "The other way round."

"What?"

The play was about a seamstress who had to choose between two lovers, a poor artist and a rich financier, and she chose the artist.

"Make her a widow with a crippled daughter," said Jem. "She marries the rich bloke to give the daughter security. Great farewell scene with the artist."

Mr Stephen scribbled CAPITAL! And when we told the Admiral he banged the floor with his wooden leg.

"I can turn a silly couplet," said Tom, "but I can't write a scene like that."

"Make it up," said Jem.

"Make it up?"

"Act it as though it is happening to you two."

Which we did, and Jem scribbled as we spoke. Tom would burst out with something and then stop because he thought it was a stupid thing to say. But, of course, the fact that he stopped was perfect and I remembered the Mail coach farewell that I had watched with Mrs Whatshername, and how she had made me think about it. From the start, the stage picture and the emotion in the space between Tom and me was part of it.

Not that we expected very much. We thought that what we did was adequate, and would serve its purpose before we essayed the serious business of Mr Wareham's Hamlet, and so forth.

Then Mr Stephen grunted, shifted and with great emphasis scribbled the words RATHBONE GOD DAMN HIS EYES HE OWES ME TWENTY GUINEAS, to suggest that our comedian acquaintance should play the older lover, and Jem said "I don't like the title, either."

"Why not?"

"I wouldn't go to see a play called Henrietta."

"What would you go to see?"

"The Price of Love," said Jem, "and don't set it in England. Keep it in Paris."

Our next discussion was financial. Elaborate scenes such as earthquakes, burning buildings and real water into which plunged the likes of Carlos the Dog had been the rage for decades, but we could only afford one location and I suggested that we set the whole play in a park.

"Tuileries Gardens, by golly!" clapped Tom, and said that we could do an outdoor ball scene at night, with lanterns, and statues that come to life and danced.

If this was implausible, so was the way in which everybody

kept meeting in the park, and my idea worried me as much as Mr Rathbone worried about playing a character who was not funny. But he reckoned that the play was so bad that it would come off after a couple of days, so that to forgo some of his salary was an easy way to pay off his debt.

His pessimism did not help matters, although Jem and Mr Stephen did make use of it.

London Green Rooms had become more than places of rest for the actors. In establishments where it was known that the actresses would be available to meet amorously inclined gentlemen the Green Room was a sort of market, written about as such in Guide Books to the city's night life, and a disgrace to our calling against which we still battle.

In the more serious theatres the Green Room would be open, through influence and friendships, to journalists and literary persons. Had not Tom met Mr Charles Dickens in the Green Room at Drury Lane? He had, and journalists of a lesser sort visited the Fitzroy.

Jem liked them. They appealed to his raffish side, and his to them. Our actresses did flirt, I must admit, and there was racy talk, and Jem grinned and seemed to be telling secrets. He was the originator of the rumours that he wanted the scandal sheets to print, and Mr Rathbone's misgivings became a story. How would the veteran comedian fare in a tragic role? Not too tragic, of course, because he won the girl. But would it herald a new career? Or could it destroy an old one?

CHAPTER THIRTY-FOUR

Thin stuff, which stirred up a sort of public interest but did nothing to lessen our fears. The dress rehearsal went like clockwork, always a bad sign, and sure enough our opening night was spluttery. It began badly when two musicians turned up drunk and had to be sent home, and Tom's performance was nervous and snatching.

This, I knew, was when anxiety and the temptation to take charge could run away with me. I looked both Tom and Mr Rathbone in the eye and saw them waver. Relax, I told myself. Make sure that what you do yourself is clear. Listen with intensity to what the other actors say, and the audience will listen with you. Open your heart.

Moment by moment Tom responded, but there was still the audience.

London audiences were as noisy as those I was used to, but in a less boozy sort of way. They were more opinionated. There were raucous young bloods with money in the Pit and working people with very little in the Gallery, and often their sympathies differed, and they called for different tunes at the end.

In candlelit theatres the smoke was troublesome but one could see the audience and know where there was hostility. With the gaslight that was more difficult. It glared and the audience was a blur, but I embraced them as well as I could, and they seemed less restive. As we came to the end Tom and I were in the wings and stared at each other like soldiers in the respite of a battle. We knew that in an early scene we had jumped and left out at least two minutes of dialogue. But no-one had noticed, and this gave us courage, I think.

"Right," I said, "Come on!" and he ran on. He turned. Would I come to elope with him? I ran into his hungry arms.

But I had made up my mind and told him, and sent him away, my back towards him as he left. Then I turned to face my future as the curtain descended but I did not notice it and began to walk.

Then there was a roar like an explosion. Was it thunder? Would there be rain? I gathered my shawl over my head but stagehands grinned and pointed. I was not in the street outside the park, the Rue de Rivoli I suppose, but in the dark backstage clutter, and the audience was on its feet, stamping, yelling, calling my name and Tom's, and it was Mr Rathbone who took my fingers and drew me to the glare, where he released me, and I stood amid the clamour, thrown flowers and coins and waving handkerchiefs of our success and fame.

CHAPTER THIRTY-FIVE

Is it true that actors become the rage in plays that are silly or inferior? I suppose it is. Mr Wareham and I had caught a fancy of which we were unaware, which made us the talk of the town, and brought interesting visitors to the Green Room, such as Mr Browning, who writes verses, and Mr Dickens himself, all energy and jokes and questions. He and Jem are now firm friends, and runners in the Great Fancy Waistcoat Handicap – the handicap being that some of us are blinded by the brightness. Mr Dickens brings with him troops of friends, among them moon-faced Mr Forster who will talk an actor's hind legs off about the play and their performances: I have to confess that I do not listen very hard to his suggestions. And lesser writers came, hoping to be commissioned, or with ideas for Afterpieces, which they seem to like because it is quick and easy money for them.

Soon Mr Wareham and I were indeed Romeo and Juliet, Hamlet and Ophelia, Macbeth and Lady Macbeth, and even Antonio and Portia, this last with Mr Rathbone as a far from convincing Shylock. Within a season our Fitzroy set a new and more realistic fashion in Shakespeare. Then we triumphed on our tour to Bristol and there was talk of Paris, where theatre is held in such high regard, and then we were at work again.

On stage there was magic, but at Admiral Wood's, backstage and in such eating houses as women could enter my heart became heavy, and my nerves ragged. Tom relied on me. But why could he not see what I felt? Why did he deny his own feelings? I determined not to wait longer, but to test him. I selected a pleasant enough young sketch author and flirted with him. He responded. There were close conversations, and very soon physical intimacies.

I enjoyed myself. It was a rehearsal for what real love could be, but when Tom showed neither jealously nor any signs of awareness I began to feel ridiculous, and angry with myself. I must dictate my own life I decided, and on the night that I dropped the poor sketch writer I came out of the theatre and said to Jem "Buy me a sandwich."

There were always street sellers with trays of food and hot drinks for the crowds, and we stood in a doorway with mustardy ham sandwiches and a sausage for Trafalgar.

"I can't go on at the Admiral's," I said. "Work's one thing, but seeing the same people all the time is too much."

What I meant was that if seeing Tom all the time was too much, the nights when he did not appear were worse, and worst of all the nights when he did appear but with some girl in tow.

"You've not lost heart, have you?" said Jem.

"No. Not altogether. But I need some room of my own."

"You mean we're too old to go on sharing?"

"Well, we are, aren't we?"

Even in London, I thought, where ten people can be crammed into one damp cellar. Jem smiled, his little smile that keeps secrets, and still reminds me of Father.

"And what's more," he said, "you're no longer nobbut a mill girl, are you?"

I was not. I had even become a sort of lady, and the Admiral had recommended me to his late wife's dressmaker in Regent Street, and a bonnet-maker near Hanover Square, and even a glove maker in an Arcade.

"We've saved and saved and been cautious, haven't we?" I said, "So now we can afford it. Can't we?"

"Just about," he said.

"St John's Wood," I said. "A lease on a little villa."

"When did you decide?"

"This evening. Second interval."

"Because of the sketch writer?"

I tossed my head. The sketch-writer was never important. Tom was, and his behaviour that night had been the limit.

"Coughing and nose-dribbling again. Rude to the other actors. Not looking at me even in the love scene."

"Again?" said Jem.

"Again. I said 'For God's sake take your linctus,' and d'you know what he said? He said 'I don't have a spoon.' I said 'Don't be so pathetic.'"

"What did he do?"

"He took a swig from the bottle."

Jem looked at me in a very particular way.

"What? What's the matter?"

"Nothing," he said. "A villa. St John's Wood. Perfect. Leave it to me."

We walked home. Jem was silent, which was unusual for him. We reached the square. Trafalgar trotted ahead and waited on the doorstep. I stopped and said "Come on. What is it? What haven't you told me?"

"Nothing."

"Jem!"

"Nothing!"

But he saw how exasperated I was, and sighed. "I think that we were right," he said. "I think his money does come from a woman."

"Who?"

He shrugged. He wasn't sure. Was it better that I did not press him? I decided that for the moment it was.

"Thank you," I said. "Let's go in."

He did not move.

"What?" I said.

The gas light hissed. The city rumbled. The gardens and the grass in the square were in deep shadows.

"Come on, Jem. What? What is it?"

"It isn't cough linctus," he said. "It's laudanum. Mr Wareham's an opium addict."

CHAPTER THIRTY-SIX

How blind we are, when we do not wish to see. But now I saw again, and understood, the grin of the apothecary and the tablets on his counter, the nervousness, the evasions, headaches, moments of stage-fright, bursts of energy, captivating visions and Tom's look, when he would search my face for an answer but had not voiced the question. Do you suspect? Do you know? What would you think if you did know?

Well, now that I did know I felt stupid. I was a fool. How many others knew when I did not? Did they smile at my ignorance? How long had Jem known? Why hadn't he told me?

And in any case, what *is* an opium addict? Many people die in pain for one reason or another, and many of them take drops of laudanum. Laudanum is a solution of opium in alcohol, and I saw Mr Whatshisname take it when he damaged his wrist in a stage fall. The apothecary's tablets had been different strength of opium, one two and three grains, I knew, and I had seen actresses take a grain when their menstrual pains were savage. And I knew, but pretended that I did not know, that mill women would on a Saturday night buy a grain if they could not afford alcohol.

I knew that everywhere people drank to obscure the misery of their lives, yet Tom's life was one that most people would envy. Often he did not behave well, but it was always exciting to be with him, and he was a success. Did it matter that he was what Jem called an opium addict? How much did

Jem know about it anyway? If opium eased some pains or mental torment, why had Tom not asked me for help? Why had he shut me out? Why was it a secret? Or had he tried to show me, in the apothecary's shop, and I been too young to see?

I understood why he had left Mr Swallow and sought London. But why had he done it so deceitfully, and damaged everybody else, and then called me to be with him as though nothing had happened?

Oh, yes, I did imagine that I knew why he had done that, because I was still in love with him, but I was angry because I had been told nothing, and the longer I lay awake that night the more angry I became.

I must have it out with him, I decided. I must force his heart open, and make him rely on me in life as he did on the stage. If I could do that, and he responded, everything would be well. Did I sleep? For an hour or two, until in the grey light I rose, splash-washed, dressed and went down two flights of stairs before anyone was awake, even the cook, and burst into Tom's room, which was an untidy mess, clothes and books and dirty crockery everywhere, and shook him awake.

"What? What? Polly? What are you doing...?"

"What does it look like?"

"My bed? Darling, I don't think of you in that way..."

I was so angry I hit him.

"Stop it! Stop it!"

He gripped my wrists. I shouted. No words. Just a noise. He shook me.

"You'll wake the bloody house!"

"I don't care."

I yelled again. There was a bang and a clatter outside. One of the other actors. "What's wrong? What's happening?"

"We're having a discussion," yelled Tom, "so bugger off!"

The actor persisted and came in.

"It doesn't sound like a discussion to me and anyway…"

"Bugger off!" I echoed.

It was the first time in my life that I used such an expression, and I was so surprised that although I was weeping I started to laugh.

"Oh," said the actor, "it's you, Polly. Sorry." And he went.

"What you can do now," said Tom, "is explain exactly why the hell you've …"

"Not me. You, Why the hell you—"

"Woken up the whole house and made us look—"

"Told me lies and never trusted me when—"

"Lies?"

"Lies! Years and years of lies!"

Silence. Then he said "Turn your back."

"What?"

"Turn your back!"

"I certainly will not."

He took off his nightshirt and I did turn, although I glimpsed his nakedness and it was beautiful.

"You can't shame me Tom whatever your name is and I won't—"

"What's this about, Polly?"

I turned back. He was in his trousers.

"You're an opium addict! That's what this is about!"

"Don't be ridiculous."

"Why didn't you tell me? Why don't you trust me?"

"Tell you? You were a child. What would you have done?"

I picked up a shoe and threw it. There were more voices outside, Trafalgar barking, and the Admiral booming from the hallway. The most important conversation of my life had become a farce.

"How could you? How could you? How could you?"

For the first time he folded his arms around me, but as an

uncle would embrace a niece, and he walked me to the door, down the stairs, past all the staring people, and with Trafalgar following, out of the house. He draped his greatcoat around me and I said "Don't you know I love you?"

"I do," he said.

"Where are we going? Why are we out here?" I said.

We sat on a half built wall. He held my hand and said "What you must understand is that I am in complete control of everything I do, and that what opium has shown me is the treasure locked away in all our minds and feelings."

He grinned, a deathly sort of grin, and seemed to both pity me and ask for sympathy.

There are so many things about your history that I do not know, I thought, and that I have never sought to know, and now may never do so, because what difference would it make? You know that I love you but have not responded. I saw Jem in the doorway. What would he ask, I thought, and said it.

"What have you done with all your money?"

"Money? What money?"

"The money you've made in the theatre?"

"What have you done with yours?" he snapped.

"Saved it. We're leaving here. We want our own house."

"You mean you're walking out on me?"

"No. We want a home again."

"That's pathetic."

"Why don't you have a home? Even Mr Stephen has a home."

"East Indian opium," he said, "which is the best, and there is no sense in having anything but the best – like alcohol. If you have the best it won't harm you – East Indian opium costs a pound sterling for three grains. But when you consider the inspiration it gives me, how would you spend the money?"

This is topsy-turvy, I thought, and said "I'm cold now. I'm going inside."

"No. No, don't do that. Stay. Talk to me."

But I was exhausted. It was too much for me. I knew nothing, and yet I knew too much, and needed time to decide what it meant.

CHAPTER THIRTY-SEVEN

Before the end of the week Jem found us a part-furnished villa and we moved in. It was a miracle: our own home after so many years, and more privacy than we had ever enjoyed. Then our excitement made us laugh at ourselves, because we realised that we were unprepared. Half the things we needed we did not possess and we did not have any real idea of how to look after ourselves. For years we had bivouacked, as it were, like luckier versions of the children we saw asleep in the street when we walked home from the theatre.

But a house with front steps and a door-knocker and a garden was not a theatre wagon. What did people do in a house? How did they use all the rooms? Who would wash, clean, cook, empty the grates and lay fires and deal with the tradesmen while we were at the theatre? Who would be there when coal was delivered? Who would walk down the street to fetch water?

"We'll advertise," said Jem. "Isn't that what people do?"

"Yes, and too many engage persons who are not to be relied upon."

"Good people have references. Don't they?"

"Besides," I said, and this thought weighed upon me, "we're not millionaires, are we? We're not the masters."

"Well after a fashion we are," said Jem, "even when we don't like what they do."

Oh dear! The difficulties of a more complicated life, and of becoming private and respectable!

"But I think I know the person," I said. "I think that I know what to do."

"What? Who?"

"I'll ask her," I said.

"Her?"

Look at folk's eyes, Mother always said. Read their faces. So and so for instance. So and so's a wrong 'un. No, no, Father would say. You can trust so and so. Mother would always purse her lips, and months or even years later be proved right. It was so and so who told the military about Father. So I came to do what Mother did, and look into faces, and prided myself on good guesswork. But now I had looked into Tom's face. How could I have missed what was there? Am I fool for love? What if I am wrong about this next person?

Not that I confessed this to Jem, although his "Right, then. Let's see what happens" cheered me up, and I went that afternoon to the dressmakers in Regent Street, where the person I was after was in charge of the workroom.

Her name was Charity, and one did not meet her often, but she would be called to watch in silence when Madame Blanche indicated a particular problem or effect. Madame Blanche herself was delighted when popular actresses wore her clothes, and would no more want to lose my goodwill than I hers, but I did want to lure away one of her best employees.

I decided that the way to do this was to make Madame herself a party to my predicament and once inside the establishment, which was more like a fashionable salon than a shop, I sank into a chair, sighed with relief at the perfume of the flowers, and said that I wanted to think about some sort of house robe.

Madame Blanche made suggestions but I did not reply. I acted like a person who was tired and distracted.

"Ma chere," said Madame. "May I presume?"

"Please."

"You are unwell? Un mal du jour?"

"No," I said. "Not that. No, no."

"Whatever I can do," she said.

I hesitated. Then I spoke. It was not difficult, because in Madame's presence I always felt that I was a girl of promise but little experience, when she was a woman who had seen most things, suffered many, and could be trusted.

I explained about our house and the comic difficulties it caused. I was sheepish and my arms and legs were all over the place. This she noticed, and I straightened my back.

"I try to live up to you," I said.

She was flattered and smiled.

"What is de rigeur in your situation," she said, "is a housekeeper."

I swallowed and nodded.

"Tell me," she said.

"I want Charity," I said.

"Charity? My Charity? Charity in the atelier?"

"Yes."

"My God," she said. Then she surprised me. She clapped her hands and laughed and said "You remind me of myself, Miss Polly Bowler."

"But I need to see her properly," I said. "I need to be sure."

She cocked her head, a very French sort of gesture, and we went into a fitting-room. Madame draped fabrics over me. Charity and a seamstress watched. Then Charity and I were alone. I looked her in the eye. We each smiled and almost laughed. My instinct was correct, and at the same time I knew that I had found what the odd happenings of my life had so far denied me – a reliable female soul mate of my own generation.

That Charity was a few years older and already a widow made no difference. She came from our part of the North, and had gone to London when her husband took a situation.

Then he died of cholera, which was as much as I knew.

Tall, dark, sallow, deep passions present but contained, she looked me back and said "Do you want something? What is it?" I explained.

"Yes," she said. "But I'm not alone."

"Not alone?"

"I have a child. Did Madame never say?"

Before I could answer Madame returned. Had she been eavesdropping? I would have done myself, in the circumstances.

"What a child needs is a Mother at home," she said, "not a shared room and strangers. N'est ce pas?"

I had been played at my own game by a shrewd woman. Yet we all gained, and within another week Jem and I had a housekeeper who engaged a skivvy, and a bright little family in the shape of two-year-old Robert, whom Trafalgar adored.

CHAPTER THIRTY-EIGHT

Postpone a decision and events will take it for you. "Do you want to stop working with Tom?" Jem asked me. "Because if you do you can't until next season."

"I don't know what I want," I said.

Like Mrs Whatshername, I was the one they gossiped about, but not to my face, and could affect to ignore things. Then one night, Tom missed a performance.

Jem went out front, made a speech of apology that the audience hissed, and someone understudied. It could have happened to any one of us, we pretended, and although Mr Stephen was gloomy everything was normal again until a Monday evening.

Tom was drowsy and all over the place. Once he looked round for a prompt and when it did not come at once abused the prompter, which the audience did not like, and at the end some booed him.

"I'm fine," he said afterward. "It's this headache. I'm fine. Leave me alone. I know what I'm doing."

"I'm not sure that you do," I said.

"I mastered the art years ago. Once every month. Plan it all out."

"Plan what out?"

"The opera."

"Opera?"

"Covent Garden. The Season. Select a night. Take a few grains beforehand. You've no concept of how the music sounds."

"But this isn't listening," said Jem. "This is being on stage yourself."

"Then afterwards, of course…"

"Afterwards?"

"Voyage. The West End. Crowds. Speak to people. Stand at the top of glaciers…."

When we were home Jem said "We need a new actor."

"We're not the management," I said.

"I'll talk to Mr Stephen."

"He's not the management, either. Tom's the management."

It was Charity who talked about love. Did I still love Tom? How deeply? Would he ever admit that he loved me in return? Was I sure that he did? Tell the truth. Had he ever hit me?

I was convinced that I could save him, I said, and that whatever it was that he missed in life I could provide.

Charity was silent, but pressed my hand.

I was not called to rehearse until the next afternoon, when I arrived to be told that Tom was missing. He had not returned to the Admiral's and could not be found. A doctor's certificate affirming Mr Wareham's indisposition was in the possession of the management, said stickers that Jem had printed and pasted where he could, but journalists in the Green Room sniffed problems and rumours spread. Mr Stephen hired a better actor than the understudy and he was sent on with the book, but audiences fell and we were in trouble.

No one had seen Tom, not at the Admiral's, nor the Argyle Divan nor any of the taverns that he went to. Then after a couple of weeks Jem said, "I think I know where he is."

"Where?"

"You can't go there," he said.

"Why not?"

"I can take a stagehand."

"What d'you mean, I can't—?"

Charity was at the table with us, and Jem explained. Tom's financial backer, he said, was almost certainly a Mrs Williams.

"Mrs William?"

"Yes."

"Never heard of her."

"No."

"Who is she?"

He glanced at Charity. They had discussed this, I saw.

"She owns an Introduction House," he said.

"What's an – ?" I began, but I stopped. I thought of a further question but did not ask that, either. I knew what an Introduction House was. An Introduction House let rooms by the night or day or hour to women who met men there, and were paid for sexual favours. Or sometimes the pair were adulterers, and sometimes, even, casual girls were lucky, and became companions.

"Where is it?" I said.

"Marble Arch," said Jem. "Just down the road, really."

"Do you know the address?"

They did.

"We'll go at once," I said.

Jem wanted to argue but Charity stopped him. On an impulse we held our hands in a ring and squeezed.

CHAPTER THIRTY-NINE

It was Charity's idea that we should not bang on the front door but go like tradesmen to the back. "Not that we're ashamed," she said, "but why embarrass the clientele?" How did they know about this, I asked. One of the actors, said Jem. One of the actors went to a girl there. Is Mrs Williams Tom's girl? Who is she? What's she like? "More like his Mother," said Jem. His Mother? "That age," said Jem.

We told our cab to wait and walked down the lane. The yard gate was undone and the back kitchen door open so we walked in. It was so simple that it was ridiculous.

There was a roaring fire in a range and a maid was startled and cried out, at which a bruiser in a waistcoat clattered down the stairs. He had a shaven head and fumbled a knuckleduster onto his fist. Then he gaped. We were not a threat, he realised.

"Good day, sir," said Jem. "We're colleagues of Mr Wareham and anxious to discover his state of health."

The bruiser hesitated. Then he turned, because a small grey-haired woman with twinkly eyes had followed him so quietly that we had not at first noticed.

"Mrs Williams?" said Jem. "How are you, ma'am? Pleased to meet you."

She looked us over and gestured for us to sit at one end of the scrubbed table. At the other end the skivvy made what looked like mince pies.

"Have I the pleasure," said Mrs Williams, "of addressing Miss Bowler?"

I smiled.

"I admire your work," she said. "I take a box. Have you noticed me?"

"The footlights," I said. "I can't see very much at all."

"Of course. In my day it was candles."

"Your day?"

"I was competent," she said, "but never as good at you. I'm sorry you had to come in here like coalmen but I suppose it makes sense. What can I do for you?"

"Is he here?" said Jem.

The bruiser had poured little glasses of cordial. Mrs Williams inclined hers in a toast and said "Are you the little business person?"

"I am," said Jem.

"He admires you."

"I admire him," responded Jem, "but it wears thin."

She flicked her eyes at the bruiser, who disappeared up the stairs.

"Can he work?" said Jem.

"See for yourself. His clothes were filthy. He must have been lying in mud. At least he came in through the yard, like you."

I wanted to ask: has he talked about me? What has he said? How much do you know about me? Why has he run away from me? But Charity held my hand in a warning grip, and in the silence Jem indicated the skivvy and said "Mince pies?"

"Gentlemen adore them out of season," said Mrs Williams. "Don't ask me why."

She looked at my hand in Charity's. Her eyes were cold as well as bright, I realised.

"I can't give him any more money, Mr Hindle," she said to Jem. "Or should I say, I won't."

"I'm not sure I would either," said Jem.

"He had a very good education," she said, as a sort of afterthought. "But I suppose you know that?"

"We don't know very much at all," I said.

"No," she said. "Perhaps not a bad thing, eh?"

Feet sounded on the stairs and there was Tom. He was as white as a man with a cancer and his clothes were new, random and very clean. He struck a pose like a character coming on stage.

"So," he said, "you're the famous Charity!"

"Charity is as charity does, Mr Wareham," she said. "Very pleased to meet you."

"My God, Polly," he said, "She's all smouldering passion underneath, what? And before I forget, some chap left these trousers I'm wearing in one of the rooms. Would you believe it?"

They were checked, and very smart.

"I mean, how did he get home without them, and what did his wife say?"

Impossible not to be amused, and Mrs Williams had a pale smile as she looked at him. Afterwards Charity said, "She's his Mother. I'm sure she's his Mother. Same eyes, did you notice?"

We did, but when we asked him he denied it, so that we were never sure, not even to this day.

CHAPTER FORTY

He was cured for ever, he said. He had rolled in Thames mud, been pick-pocketed, almost lost his reason, seen Marco Polo flying through the air over London Bridge, gone into a druggist, stolen three pellets and run out, been chased and escaped his pursuers by jumping over a haystack. Don't you believe me?

No, we said. Are you fit to go on stage?

Yes, he said, and did, and was magical as Hamlet. When he said "the readiness is all" it was as though he had arrived at great wisdom. The audience stamped and roared as we took our calls. I squinted at the boxes but if Mrs Williams was there I could not discern her, and Jem never saw her come in.

It was exhilarating, a roaring furnace of the public's love, but it was the last time. The truth is that he was taking about eighty small teaspoons of laudanum a day, which is to say eight thousand grains of the higher strength, at a cost of a hundred pounds sterling.

This was more than the theatre's profits, more than what he stole or borrowed from women and the Admiral, or took from the Wardrobe and Property Store to some pawnbroker. It was more than he was found to have taken from money lenders, with promissory notes on the theatre's future earnings.

Within days the money went, and with it his ability to buy the drug. He lost confidence and was desperate. Sweats and cramps overtook him, constipation doubled him over in agony.

Jem and Mr Stephen were in despair. They hid what cash

they could, but it was not long before bailiffs appeared and seized what remained of Tom's possessions. Then there was a Court Order against him, to confine him to the Debtors Prison at the Marshalsea.

"He'll die in there," I said. "We can't let them. We must hide him."

We bought laudanum to make him normal if only for a while, and I took him in a chaise and lost all dignity. "I love you. Why do you do this? Trust me, I can save you."

"No, you can't," he said. "You can't."

We arrived at our house and he went into the garden, where Robert and Trafalgar romped around him. He was bent like an old person. "I know what we need," he said. "We need some jellied eels for supper."

"Wait," I said. "Wait till Jem comes home."

He said he would, and Charity and I went to make up a truckle bed for him. Before we had finished Trafalgar barked and came to us, very agitated, and I knew what had happened. We ran downstairs. The front door was open, the gate closed so that Robert and Trafalgar would not follow, and Tom gone, never to return.

CHAPTER FORTY-ONE

There was no word, no rumour, no return to Mrs Williams, which we knew because Jem communicated with her, no body dragged from the river or found in the street. He was gone, consumed like so many by London's vastness, maybe, or walking to die or be redeemed in fields faraway. His debts would never be repaid, the actors and stagehands had lost their jobs, Mr Stephen moped at home all day, the theatre was dark, and our problem was what to do next.

Should we try to run the theatre ourselves? How could we, when we did not have enough money? Should we take what work we could find? Difficult, because we were mid-season, and although there were several who would have engaged me, they would not be able to do so for months. Then Jem had a brainwave.

"'The Handicapped Husband,'" he said.

"The what?"

"Mr Whatshisname's play in race week."

"You mean 'The Handicapped Suitor?'" I remembered.

"Husband's better," said Charity.

"Much better," said Jem.

"It was the one where the lover dressed as a girl and his sweetheart as a boy."

"It was."

"So who's the husband?" I said. "Is he the girl's Father?"

"Yes."

"But he's not handicapped. Is he? He's not in love with anyone. Not as far as I remember."

"Well," said Jem, "we can change all that."

"You mean rewrite it?"

"Yes."

"You and me?"

"No. We'll hire a writer."

"Who?"

"What about that chap you had a romance with?"

Charity stared from one to the other.

"No," I said. "Certainly not. Never. Anyway he's not – I mean the last I heard he was writing silly songs for the East End."

Jem looked disappointed.

"Jem," I said. "Why have you had this idea?"

"Astley's" he replied.

I understood at once. Astley's Theatre is across the river at Westminster Bridge Road, and is a large arena that presents equestrian spectacles.

"Horses," I said.

"Horses?" repeated Charity, and Jem grinned, and I thought: a play about horse racing in which a girl disguises herself as a boy. Something went flash! through my mind.

"In that case," I said, "this is what we'll do—" and out I burst with my idea.

CHAPTER FORTY-TWO

My suggestion was rash and even dangerous but it had nothing to do with Mr Wareham. It would take me away from him and create something new and my own. Jem and Charity were excited, as were Astley's, when Jem sold them the idea.

They proposed a date two months hence. We had misgivings but accepted. We were used to plays being rewritten and rehearsed in a few weeks. That was not the problem. The problem was the task that I had set myself.

My idea was that the heroine would change places not with the stable-lad, but with a jockey. She would ride in the big race, and urge her mount to victory.

Astley's arena is big enough for horses to be ridden at full gallop, and in a staged race they would run in the order demanded by the story. Would I, who had never ridden except at a plod on old Fletcher's back when someone walked at his head, learn to match old jockeys and experienced riders for skill? That was the question, and it was not answered without many falls and bruises.

If I had broken bones we would have been forced to abandon, I suppose, and I did once put my shoulder out, but I worked with the same horse, who was Sweetheart by nature as well as name, and my luck held.

Sweetheart's groom was a spindly cross-eyed twelve-year-old called Threepence. He slept with the horses and although he could neither read nor write made up his own rhyming slang, and my riding master was Corporal Cleverley, a one-armed wizard who said very little but every word of it to the point.

Some of the other riders were boys, and some ex-jockeys too old or overweight to ride in races. There were also Astley's equestrian actors, who rode well enough to get themselves into position to act, and one or two side-saddle actresses. Some riders were envious of me, and one tried in the race rehearsals to force Sweetheart to crush me against the barrier. I rode astride in breeches, of course, and could have smashed my knee, but Sweetheart was too smart a performer to be caught.

Corporal Cleverley observed this, and said nothing. But before the next run he nodded with meaning at two of his particular cronies, and how they did it I do not know, but the offender was soon tipped off his own horse, kicked by a hoof as he rolled in the sawdust, and thereafter behaved himself.

"My big toe!" said Threepence as he helped me down, "He ate his ballyhoo!"

Which meant, I think, "There you go, he met his Waterloo!" Ballyhoo, the real Waterloo, that is, was where the Corporal went to the farm, lost his arm, that is, in General Ponsonby's charge.

So it was very matey in the daytimes, when the Corporal sent out for whelks and oyster pies, and the actress riders told blue stories at which they guffawed like men. But at night I went home saddle-sore, bruised and aching.

Trafalgar would lie in front of the fire in my bedroom grate, and Charity would fill the hip bath and sponge me. On the Corporal's advice I had all sorts of oils and ointments from a gentleman's shop in one of the Arcades. Charity would rub linament into the bruises I could not reach, and we would talk quietly about our feelings, and what we thought about love.

CHAPTER FORTY-THREE

Charity's husband been the perfect person for her. She had met him by chance, when they bumped into each other on a snowy Manchester street, and she could not imagine any other person who would suit her more. Then he had died, and young Robert was more like Charity herself than his Father. Did she look for or want another man? She did not, particularly. "I'm lucky," she said. "I've had something perfect, and that can't last, can it, even when people stay together."

"I don't know," I said, "I've not had the chance to find out."

"What about your Father and Mother?"

"They were strong together," I said, and told her about the night-time football. "But something did go wrong, I suppose."

"What?"

"I don't know."

"Maybe nothing they could help."

"How d'you mean?"

"Maybe the life around him changed," she said, and I thought: that's true. It did.

Water splashed as she wrung out the sponge. Candles and firelight flickered.

"But women have always had to face hard questions, haven't they" I said, "for thousands and thousands of years?"

She held the towel for me to step out.

"I mean if we know that a man's bad," I said, "is it wrong to have his children?"

She unscrewed the ointment jar. She knew what I meant.

When she says nothing, I thought, it can mean more than when she speaks.

"I cried all night last night," I said. "I couldn't stop at all."

"Well. This shoulder must still be very sore."

But it was my heart, as well she knew. It was my heart.

"But you're a woman in twenty thousand," she said. "Don't you realise?"

I did, and it meant that I had to make life up as I went along.

"Independence," she said. "Your own money. Your own life."

"But don't you want to love again?" I said. "Don't you want to be consumed by it?"

She replaced the top of the jar.

"Why else were we born?" I said.

And we were silent, because neither of us was sure of the answer.

CHAPTER FORTY-FOUR

On the night we opened the play the rehearsed race was perfect. The brass band hit a crescendo as I passed the winning post, stood in the stirrups and took off my silk cap so that my hair streamed free and the audience realised that I was a girl. They gasped and then cheered as though it had been a real race, and a real victory like that of Cloudy Mary. Overnight the play became the rage, and because it was Astley's it brought a kind of interest that I had not experienced.

Astley's shows were about horses, and horses drew as well as riff-raff a gentrified and even aristocratic audience that was not always interested in other kinds of theatre. We would be visited in our dressing rooms by Sir Somebody This or That, and be obliged to go out front to be introduced to the Duke of Why or Whatever.

One night Threepence appeared and said "Under the gables. Sea and sands." I duly went to the stables to shake hands with some important personage, and to my amazement it was the Duke of Beverley, to whom I had refused to sell Trafalgar.

He was surrounded by a sporting life entourage: two pugilists, his professional cricketer, bookmakers, a jolly clergyman, Jimmy Muggles the jockey, believe it or not, and a buxom lady with very red lips.

The Government had fallen recently and Beverley was out of office, and looked all the merrier for it, but my heart pounded and I found it hard to hear his questions or to answer them. I need not have worried. He congratulated me with no sign of recognition. But Jimmy Muggles stared with a frown, and when the others moved on to talk to the Clowns and look at the horses who did tricks in the interval, he came back and said "It's you, isn't it? Trafalgar's Polly?"

"Yes."

"How is the old dog?"

"Still going strong. How's Cloudy Mary?"

He gestured to say that she was fine.

"She won the Oaks, didn't she?" I said.

"It changed Beverley's luck, you know."

"Cloudy Mary?"

"Not buying the dog. He always says. If he'd been selfish and insisted, he says, he'd have brought down a curse. Shall I tell him it's you?"

"No need," I said. "He knows who I am. I am Polly Bowler, aren't I?"

Which I was and wasn't, and wished I never had been, in a way, and I knew that I needed some new vain scheme to distract me. So did Jem, and he raised money from some of the wealthy men who went from Astley's to the clubs and cigar divans, and places where women were either not allowed or could not be seen and stay respectable, and he went into partnership with the devious Mr Bunn of Drury Lane, and took the lease of the Fitzroy Theatre.

"So it's up to you, Polly," he said. "You're the attraction. What do you want to do next?"

"Hamlet," I said.

"What?"

"Hamlet."

"Hamlet's a man's part"

"That's why," I said.

For a moment I thought that he might jump about and explode, like a rip-rap. But it was from excitement and not exasperation.

"A woman prince!" he said. "It's better than horse-racing! It's sensational!"

CHAPTER FORTY-FIVE

"I'll act Mr Wareham off the stage," I said to Charity. "Off the stage and out of our lives." I had been Ophelia who goes mad for lack of love, and now I would be the Prince who goes mad for – for what? I would discover, I supposed. But what I had to cope with first was the fact that if anyone was in charge of what happened on our stage it was me, and I soon realised that, although I could draw upon what Mrs Whatshername had taught me, I needed advice.

I sought it from Mr Macready. He is the main actor of our day and famous, not to say notorious, for the thoroughness of his rehearsals. I have never acted with him because his regular lady Miss Faucit, having failed some years ago to woo him from his wife, always makes sure that no-one else will have the opportunity. Even so, for any woman a conversation with Mr Macready is like talking to a mountain. Answers come from high up, and very far away.

But his knowledge of plays and our work is as unrivalled as his advice is sound, and I was grateful. What he said helped our production to keep its shape, even if the main ingredient in its success was the novelty of seeing a woman carry off the part of the Prince. Another was that we were endorsed by royalty.

Perhaps the first among the influences that have made the theatre seem less disreputable in recent years is the interest in it shown since her accession by the young Queen and Prince Consort. They have attended numerous performances, and the custom is that the cast are lined up afterwards in the foyer, to be presented to them.

When it was my turn to be presented I was startled to find the Queen much smaller than me, as small as Jimmy Muggles, in fact, and although I wore a man's doublet and hose I curtseyed. At the silliness of this she began to giggle, but converted it to a regal smile. I saw the beauty of her complexion, and the firmness in her eye.

Prince Albert was interested to learn that for the duels I had learned to fence, and their Royal Highnesses had friends with them. One of these was a tall man with a grey-gold beard and blue eyes, who would have talked to me, I thought, but had to keep pace with the party as it moved along the line. All the men, I said later to Charity, had stared at my legs in their black hose. "Well," she said, "they're pretty good and long, aren't they?"

CHAPTER FORTY-SIX

Another thing came from Hamlet and my discussions with Mr Macready. He mentioned them to Mr Dickens and their artist friend Mr Maclise, and Mr Dickens suggested to Mr Maclise that he should paint my portrait. Pictures of popular actors, often in costume, are afterwards engraved, and the engravings sell everywhere and make money for the artist. Mr Maclise I did not know but I had heard well of him, and agreed to sit.

He is dark, Irish, very confident, and talks a lot in a Cork accent in which everything seems to be said rapidly through clenched teeth, so that I understand about six words in ten. But what he says is always enjoyable and when I sat for him, not as Hamlet, but as myself, in dark silks and a Norwich shawl, he would bombard me with questions such as "Are they mad folk in the theatre then? Are they now? Would you say that they are, would you?"

But before I could tell him about our actress Mrs Barker who keeps two rabbits in her dressing room, or Mr Howarth, who wears his lucky undershirt on first nights, and for twenty-five years has refused to wash it, Mr Maclise would be off with more questions.

"Painters, did you say? Are painters mad? Miss Polly, painters can be very mad, now, but fiddlers are worse. There's blind Irish fiddlers as mad as they come. Or would the maddest be old Mr Turner now? What would you say? Would you like to see him? Keep your head still. Would you like to see Mr Turner? Blink if you would. Well, I tell you what. I tell you what, Miss Polly. I'll take you to the Varnishing Day."

Which he did. Varnishing Day at the Royal Academy is when the Annual Exhibition receives its final touches, and those in the know are admitted before the wider public. Mr Turner, not much bigger than Jimmy Muggles but stockier with the years, shabby and ramshackle, spectacles at the end of his nose, and watched by people who seemed afraid of him, stood some distance from a painting and dabbed at it with a very long brush.

The painting depicted a storm, and it took my breath away, because it was like days on the road with Mr Swallow, when we trudged over the tops and the weather was a dark whirl in our faces, in our eyes and mouths and ears, but despite the misery was splendid, a display of something awesome, because in the depths of the snowflakes there was light.

"Is it yourself, Mr Turner?" said Mr Maclise, "Is it yourself up to your tricks again?"

"Daniel," said Mr Turner, "go away."

"Will you meet Miss Bowler, then? Will you doff your brush to Miss Polly Bowler?"

"Never heard of her."

"I've never heard of you," I said, "until the day before yesterday."

Mr Turner stopped. He looked at me, and his eyes were more penetrating than anyone's before or since. His grin was very saucy for an old man, I thought.

"How much is the picture?" I said. "It's wonderful. I'll buy it."

"Don't be silly," he said, and returned to what he was doing. But later he did let me buy it, and it is here in the room with me now, as strange as the weather it describes.

Then on that day we stepped aside to respect Mr Turner's need for space, and I almost banged into someone. I looked up and was surprised. It was the man with the grey-gold beard who had accompanied the Queen and Prince Albert to see my Hamlet.

"Miss Bowler," he said, with an almost silent click of his heels and a bow. He's foreign, I thought, and in the same instant saw that once again he had to follow a party who were ahead of him. His gesture made fun of himself. "One day," he said, "we shall converse. I promise."

CHAPTER FORTY-SEVEN

At home Charity was agog to hear about the Varnishing, and when I came to describe my chance encounter she said "He's what? He's who? Are you sure?"

"Of course I'm sure."

"He's an Archduke? He's the brother of a king?"

"You saw him at the theatre," I said.

"How old is he?"

"You saw him. How old would you say?"

"Did he touch you?"

"What?"

She gestured.

"Of course he didn't touch me. There were people. Anyway, why would he?"

"What did you think?"

"When?"

"On your way home."

"I didn't think anything."

"How about a marmalade sandwich?" she said, and we went to the kitchen to make them and put on the kettle. Eventually she said "No, I don't suppose you will see him again." And before I could protest she added, "All the same. You do have to think about it."

"Think about what?"

She took a bite of her sandwich. I waited.

"Robert came out with some new words today," she said.

"What are they?"

"Oh ... Dust pan. And Nicolson."

This was a very broad hint. Our neighbour on one side

was a barrister's clerk and his family, and on the other the pretty Miss Nicolson, who adored Robert and bought him wooden toys. Miss Nicolson was paid for by a married City merchant who visited her twice a week.

"You have to think about what you'd do," said Charity.

"You mean, what would I do if an Archduke made an offer to keep me?"

"Yes."

"Well, I know what you'd do."

"What?"

"You'd refuse."

"I'm not sure that I would, if I liked the man, and Robert needed things."

"I don't have a Robert to look after."

She continued to study me.

"Oh for heaven's sake, Charity! An Archduke? Me? How could it happen? Why would I want it to? How could you and me live among all those grand people?"

"How did you become Polly Bowler?" she replied.

Before I could think of an answer there was a cheery door-banging and shouting as Jem arrived with an actor named Mr Morris, to whom, he explained, he had promised a bed for the night so that Mrs Morris would not discover that they had been out drinking. "I'm afraid I'm off to bed myself, Mr Morris," I said, not best pleased, but I had to listen to this, said Jem, I had to listen to what had just happened to Mr Morris in the provinces.

What happened, said Jem, and listen to this, what happened was that an actor in the company named Studland was dismissed because he stole money from everybody, but this was not the point of the story. The point of the story was that one actress was left with nothing, so Mr Morris had lent her the fare to London. They travelled together and Mr Morris thinks that he fell in love with her but he isn't sure.

"Isn't sure?"

"She talks all the time," said Mr Morris.

"And men are infuriating self-important pomposities all the time but does it stop them being welcomed as Fathers?" said Charity.

"Steady on," said Jem. "Rules of debate. Only one marmalade at a time."

It was ludicrous, and typical, I am ashamed to say, of many things that happened at that time.

Next morning Jem and Mr Morris were a mixture of the defiant and the sheepish, and we heard later that when Mr Morris got home his wife hit him on the head with a warming pan.

"Would you wallop a naughty Archduke?" said Charity.

"Never. I'd have a servant to do walloping for me," I retorted, and we laughed.

CHAPTER FORTY-EIGHT

So time passed, and all of it spent on work, at which our success did not buy pleasure but more work, more decisions, more worries, more risks, more occasions on which we had to smile and be polite, to endure boredom, and seem interested when we were not.

London and all the people in it seemed to shake with energy as though in an earthquake, and indeed there were huge excavations, and dust in the air, and mountains of rubble as space was made for the railways. On our tour we took the trains for the first time: hissing monsters, hard seats, soot-specks, and sights whizzing past.

We made money but country audiences missed most of the finer points and even in London no-one seemed sure of what they wanted the theatre to be. Neither did I. What should I play? Men? Women? Was love on stage like love in real life? I was dispirited.

When we got home it was midsummer and at least pipes had brought water to our street. We installed water closets and ran hot baths and it made us feel very up to date, although we still seemed to bicker and be bored.

Then one day Jem said "Cheer up! I know what we need! A river voyage!"

It might be an adventure, we hoped, but when we arrived at the London Bridge Steam Wharf the Thames stank like the sewer it is and thundery heat had lowered the sky and brought rain splashes, and we found ourselves stuck in a shoving mass of people half-way down the rickety stairs.

Why we had brought Trafalgar I did not know, but he

hated the stairs because he is stiff-legged now, and as more rain fell I looked down at the steamer for Greenwich. It had few seats and no cover, and people on the stairs had begun to recognise me. A woman said to her child "Go on! Touch her!" and the child put a hand that was greasy from a meat pie on my sleeve.

"Damn this," I said, "I'm leaving."

I started to push my way back up the steps. Jem with a picnic basket and Charity with Trafalgar and Robert protested, but tried to follow. Trafalgar scrambled ahead. When I reached the pavement at the top it was like bursting into fresh air even though rain fell and umbrellas popped open. I dragged Trafalgar into the first cab I saw, went home, and got into bed.

When Jem arrived he burst in and was very angry. "You left us! You left Robert! You can't leave Robert! Do you know how long we were in the rain?"

"Go away! I don't want anybody! Go away!"

"Don't carry on with me like an Italian opera prima what-not!"

I was weeping and threw a pillow at him.

"Don't smoke cigars!" I screamed. "They'll only make you smaller than you are!"

As he went he slammed the door so hard that the reverberations shook an ornament off a shelf, and it smashed.

I lay on my back and shouted "Oh! Oh! Oh!" I pummelled the bedclothes. I felt a shameful fool even though I was sure that no-one understood me. I was their drudge, hauling their wagon like old Fletcher. They made me work and fed off me, until I was as useless as my broken ornament.

Then I realised that I was still in my street clothes, took half of them off, and fell asleep. Something woke me. Thunder. Drumming rain. Why was I – oh, Lord! I remembered. I felt as heavy as lead, as we do when we have been in a quarrel and want things put right. An Italian opera prima what-not, I thought. Oh dear. They're the worst of the lot, as we all know, worse by far than even Miss Faucit. I went to sleep and when I woke again everything was fresh. Clear sunshine. Blue sky. I put on clean clothes, so that I would be new and different, and went downstairs. It was late afternoon.

Jem looked up. He was reading one of his atlases again.

"Didn't you miss lunch?" he said. "I think you did. Tea and biscuits?"

"I'm sorry," I said. "I didn't mean that about the cigars."

"It could well be true," he said. "I'm experimenting."

"You're a little beast," I said, grinning, and he said "So are you. And Charity's in the garden."

I went out. Robert was playing and because the seats were still damp, Charity stood up with him.

"I'm sorry," I said. "I was awful. I don't think I'm all that happy."

We looked at each other. She held up a finger. Wait. She snapped off a rose and gave it to me. We smiled.

I was lost in the scent of the rose when there was a clatter and a bump and Robert cried. He had fallen over.

Charity bent herself round him to give comfort and as she did so I felt a great surge in my own body and knew what ailed me. I did not want to imitate life on the stage but to create it. I needed a child of my own.

CHAPTER FORTY-NINE

I was not ill but I was exhausted. I went to bed early and slept late and was in limbo: waiting: wandering: in a sort of timelessness, which when it ended did so like a fairy-tale.

Charity had slung hammocks in the garden and we were reading aloud to each other, and keeping an eye on Robert and Trafalgar, when the maid came out, very excited, and with an envelope.

"Lor blimey, Miss Polly but – sorry, Miss Polly. Sorry Mrs Charity. But there's a coachman arrived."

"A coachman?"

She pointed. We went inside and peered. There was a gleaming equipage. Its driver was down from his box, and waiting at our gate.

The envelope was addressed to me and had a crest on the flap. I opened it, read the note inside, and felt dizzy.

"It's from him, isn't it?" said Charity.

"Yes."

"What does it say?"

I handed it to her. She scanned it.

"It's a bit short notice," she said.

"No it isn't," I decided. "Haven't I known all the time?"

"Well. Sometimes we know but don't know," she replied.

When she returned from speaking to the coachman I said "What shall I wear?"

"It won't matter to him," she said. "He'll remember but it won't matter. It'll be your way of doing things whatever it is."

"My eyes," I said. "I've got dark circles."

"We'll put on our everyday bonnets," she said, "and go as we are."

Which we did. Charity and I were very casual for an open carriage in Hyde Park, Robert had green garden stains on him, and Trafalgar was uncombed.

At the West Carriage Drive end of Rotten Row the Archduke and his groom dismounted and awaited us. The Archduke carried a paper bag.

"Fraulein Polly," he said. "Frau Charity, I presume? Young man." And he nodded at Trafalgar.

"Trafalgar," I said.

"Very good. I've a new hound at home. We can call her Hamilton."

He had a biscuit for Trafalgar, and handed the paper bag to Robert. It contained toffee apples.

"How did you know we'd all come?" I said.

It was self-evident, said his shrug, and as he handed me down from the carriage I thought: how does he know all this about us? And then: how do I know that his wife died in childbirth and that – well, how do I know what I know about him?

He consulted his watch. "Half an hour?" he asked Charity, and she said "I think so," and the coachman took her and Robert around the Park's perimeter. Trafalgar walked with us around the Serpentine.

"I'm sure," began the Archduke, "that with your memory you will soon learn German and any other tongue that takes your fancy."

"How do you know about my memory?"

"From Prince Albert, who was told by Mr Macready."

"Oh."

"The theatre on the continent can be more serious," he said. "That is, if you are still in love with acting."

"I don't know," I said. "I hope that I'm in love with you."

He stopped. He raised my two hands to his lips and kissed them.

"And what we have," he said, "is all the time in the world."

CHAPTER FIFTY

But we did not. Next day Jem and I were at the theatre to go through the books and discuss how we would continue if for a while I travelled through Europe with the Archduke. When we were satisfied, Jem sent the call boy to fetch a cab, and the boy came back and said "Stage door sir, when you're ready,"

"We're coming. Two minutes."

"That actor was here again," said the boy.

"What actor?"

"Asking for you – looking for work."

"Well, if he wants me he'll find me," said Jem.

The boy went and Jem said "Remember when I was a call boy?"

"I do," I said, "and you were usually off discovering about something else."

"Who was the Queen of Yorkshire?" he said. "Did we ever discover that?"

"Never," I said, and as we descended the stone staircase we picked up an empty beer bottle that someone had left on a half-landing, and gave it to the Stagedoor Keeper.

"You're lucky that they've not pissed in it," he said.

"Not in front of the ladies," said Jem, and we went out into the din of the street.

"There," said Jem. "Cab's a hundred yards up."

I took two steps and then he saw me. He came out of a doorway opposite and I felt another of those lurches of the heart.

"Tom," I said, "Tom Wareham, or whoever you are now."

"Studland," he said, "hadn't you heard?"

"We had," said Jem. "Bugger off."

"I love you, Polly. I always did. Couldn't admit it. Don't know why. But I've come back. Had to."

"You're a liar and we don't—"

I put my hand on Jem's arm. Tom was haggard. He shook. But he had determined to fight, I realised. To fight and overcome, or be destroyed. And I loved him, with that blind, total, stupid, ruinous love that destroys everything. The love of a person whose demand is not to need, but to be needed.

"Save me," he said, and did Jem snarl "Save yourself. Leave proper people alone"? He did, I suppose, but what I heard was "I need you. Save me. Macbeth and Lady Macbeth. We can show them. Queen of Yorkshire…"

For a mad second I thought that Jem would ask who the Queen of Yorkshire was, but he didn't. He stared, and was bewildered, and so was I. What have we achieved I thought, and what are we worth, and whose children should we bring into the world? And Tom's useless lying face stared at me.

Oh reader, oh my dear and valued reader! What would you have me decide?

THE END

www.ingramcontent.com/pod-product-compliance
Ingram Content Group UK Ltd.
Pitfield, Milton Keynes, MK11 3LW, UK
UKHW042000230426
12048UKWH00009B/449